The Dead Years

THRESHOLD

JEFF OLAH

Copyright © 2013 Jeff Olah
All Rights Reserved.

No part of this book may be reproduced, or stored in a retrieval system, or transmitted in any form or by any means, electronic, mechanical, photocopying, recording, or otherwise, without the express written permission of the publisher.

This is a work of fiction. The characters, locations and events portrayed in this book are fictitious. Any similarity to actual persons, living or dead, businesses, events, or locales is merely coincidental and not intended by the author.

Cover design by Rebecca Frank
(http://rebeccafrank.design)

. . .

Visit the author's website for free stories, behind the scenes extras and much more.
www.JeffOlah.com

ISBN-13: 978-1523830145
ISBN-10: 152383014X

BOOKS BY JEFF OLAH

The Dead Years Series:
ORIGINS
THRESHOLD
TURBULENCE
BLACKMORE
COLLAPSE
VENGEANCE
HOMECOMING
RETRIBUTION
ABSOLUTION

The Last Outbreak Series:
AWAKENING
DEVASTATION
DESPERATION
REVOLUTION
SALVATION

More Stories:
RATH
INTENT

The End of the World was Only the Beginning

1

No one knew how or where it all began. There were only rumors at first, spreading from one city to another. The infection took hold quickly. Many that became victims of the first wave were caught off guard by the unusual behavior of those infected. Millions perished with each day that passed and the number of survivors continued to dwindle as they desperately searched for places free of this hell.

The devastation was almost immediate. Law enforcement fell, utilities powered down and civilization was shattered within the first few weeks. With no structure left in the world, the few remaining sought to band together to fight and survive in this new existence.

They had no other choice...

Mason looked out over the floor in between sets and was somewhat caught off guard, and also a little amused as one of his favorite songs from high school started up through his headphones. He hadn't heard this for quite some time and figured his phone must be cycling through the deep reaches of his enormous playlist.

Just as the chorus set in, the music muted, signaling a call was coming through. Mason pulled the phone from his pocket to check who was calling. "April," he said aloud. He figured there must be something else she needed to harass him about and he wasn't going to ruin another workout just to satisfy her need to belittle him. He hit decline and lay back on the floor for another set of crunches.

Mason ran through his next set like a man on fire and lost all focus on the world around him. He often used his outside frustrations to fuel his high intensity workouts in the gym. This proved to be an effective tool in that he was able to push off his problems and at the same time get into top shape. The downside to all this was that his workouts, coupled with the time spent training clients, fueled the fire that resulted in his and April's separation three months ago.

Rolling forward and standing from his final set, Mason was surprised to see the weight room almost empty. He turned and noticed at least thirty people gathered outside the owner's office and as he got closer, he saw there was at least half that amount inside the office.

They seemed to be intently debating something as others hurried out the front exits of the gym and were headed for their cars. Mason asked one of the female on-lookers what was happening and just as she began to answer, his phone started to buzz, indicating he was getting a text message.

Again it was April.

Looking back at the woman standing directly in front of him, now appearing irritated, Mason said, "I apologize, what did you say?"

"The old folks home," she said.

"Yes..." Mason followed.

"They're killing each other... LOOK!"

Mason pushed his way through the diminishing crowd inside the office to get a glimpse of the television now directly in front of him.

The reporter standing in the hallway was in the middle of his report when he was overtaken by what appeared to be three individuals, all of whom were at least eighty years old.

Someone in the crowd said, "I am not sure what the hell they're taking, but I want some. Damn, I have never seen people that age move so fast."

The news station cut away just as the threesome overtook the reporter. The footage was disturbing in that it appeared as though they were not just attacking the reporter, but trying to devour him. The first crazed senior appeared to bite the reporter on the neck or face and just as they cut away it looked as though the others had the same intention.

The station went to a commercial and Tom the owner switched to another station covering a mysterious virus plaguing an emergency room with the same sort of crazy behavior; this time it wasn't senior citizens. The cameraperson appeared to be running from the hospital and dropped the camera just as he was trapped on all sides by the angry horde.

Mason looked over at Tom and watched as the remaining members either headed toward the doors or to the locker room, fearing the unknown. Tom stared at the screen a minute longer watching as the cameraman was torn to shreds by nothing more than the hands and mouths of the rabid individuals.

"Tom!"

"Yeah, what?" Tom said as though coming out of a fog.

"What the hell is happening?"

"How on earth would I know? It's on every damn station though... check it out."

As Tom flipped from one station to the next, every station—even the local cable channels—had coverage of these bizarre events taking place. Some of the network channels had started to go dark and this appeared to concern Tom.

"Mason, I'm closing up for the day. I need to get home; my wife is probably flipping out. I'm surprised she hasn't called yet. If you want to stay you can lock up, otherwise let's go."

"That's fine," Mason said. "I'm going to grab my bag and I'll just be a few minutes behind you."

Heading back toward the locker room, Mason turned and looked as Tom reached the front door.

"Tom, take care, I'll call you later."

Mason pulled the phone from his pocket and looked down remembering he had put April on ignore. "Great," he said.

Opening April's text, it read: Check the news, I am really scared – PLEASE CALL ME!!!

Mason sat in front of his locker and dialed April. Being the only remaining soul inside the gym felt a little creepy and not just because of the earlier images he had seen on the news. He always hated being here alone, especially when it was dead silent, and being here mid-afternoon with the place empty was just weird.

"Mason!" April answered on the forth ring.

"I'm just leaving the gym now," Mason said.

"Where are you headed?"

"Home... why?"

"Can you come here?" April asked. "I'm really scared and I need you."

"Where is Justin?" Mason asked.

"He's in school; I just checked out the window and everything is quiet."

Mason had never heard April this worried. He figured he would try to set her mind at ease. "I'm on my way to your place. Stay put and I'll be there in a few minutes."

"I will," April said, sounding a little less stressed.

"Mason?"

"Yeah?"

"I just spoke to my Dad."

"Oh yeah, what did HE have to say about this?"

"He didn't say very much, although he made me promise him that we would get out of the city... TODAY!"

2

April hung up the phone and walked to the oversized bay window in her master bedroom. The home she had purchased eight years ago with Mason was supposed to be her dream home. Instead, it now reminded her of how hard she had been on him and how much she had let her father influence those bad times.

Thinking back to the better memories they shared, she remembered that they had decided on this home in particular because it overlooked not only the elementary, but also the middle and high schools. She persuaded Mason that if they stuck to the budget she outlined, they could literally watch their son grow from kindergarten to high school. She was sure her being overprotective did nothing to help their marriage. Mason would constantly let her know she needed to "loosen the reigns," especially since Justin was only a few months shy of his fourteenth birthday.

She desperately hoped Mason would arrive

soon as she was freaked out after watching the news all day and talking to dear old dad.

"I guess we were spared," April said aloud as she looked out the window surveying both campuses, half trying to convince herself that she had nothing to worry about. No frantic people running around; in fact, the area seemed overly calm.

April made her way downstairs and into the kitchen just as the phone rang. She was sure it was Mason with some sort of an update, although upon checking the caller ID she noticed the call was coming from Justin's cell.

"Hello?" she quickly answered, trying to sounds as if she had not a care in the world.

"Mom, something weird is happening."

"What's going on?"

"All the teachers and staff were called to an emergency meeting and they haven't been back to the classrooms. It's been almost an hour now."

"Where are you?" April said.

"I walked out into the gym because the rest of the school is too loud. The other students are kind of just running around the halls. Mom, some of my friends are saying that there is a war that was started."

"Justin, I think they're just trying to scare you."

"Well, what IS going on? Why are all the teachers gone? Why haven't they come back?"

"I'm sure it's nothing. Just go back to cl…"

"Mom they're coming back, I gotta go."

April set the phone down and leaned back

against the counter. She wanted Justin home and had to talk herself out of walking across the street to get him. She knew it would embarrass him and probably her as well.

April decided she would head back to the bedroom and sit at the window and watch, that way she could ease her mind and at the same time she would be ready to move if anything changed.

Even before she reached the window, April could see both parking lots start to fill with cars. Knowing there were no performances going on at the middle school today, she knew what was happening.

These parents were just as alarmed at the events of the day as she was; they were just less concerned with what the other parents thought of them.

"Screw it." Deciding she didn't care either, she dialed Mason again to let him know she was headed to the school to bring Justin home. She figured he could help her pack a few things and as soon as Mason arrived she would try to convince him that her father had some insight and they should heed his warning and head out of town.

Mason's phone went to voicemail once again. April typically would have just hung up, although she wanted him to know where she was if he got here before she got back.

"Mason, it's me, there is some weird stuff going on over at the school. I'm going over to bring Justin home. If you get here before I get back, the front door will be unlocked...Please hurry."

Before heading out, April grabbed the

television remote and powered it up. She promised herself earlier that she would not watch any more coverage; however, she wanted to be sure there wasn't any new information.

Most of the network stations were now off the air. April flipped through the last of the local stations and came upon a disturbing feed that was playing on a loop showing a crowd of deranged people stampeding two middle aged women trying to get into the grocery store. She had to turn away and instantly hit the off button before she witnessed another second.

"What in the world is happening?"

3

April's father was a great man, sometimes too great for Mason to even stomach. He knew April loved him, but he also knew their marriage would continue to be an uphill battle as long as her father continued to add fuel to the fire.

Putting that aside, Mason knew better than to doubt this man. He knew April's father was some sort of military big shot; he just had no idea what kind. He figured it was better not to ask as it would have just led to some sort of discussion about why he couldn't measure up... it always did.

Mason dropped the phone into his backpack and headed for the exit. Walking down the row of treadmills, he made sure to turn down the lights in each section of the club. Rounding the corner and making his way out, Mason nearly tripped over the front desk chair as he couldn't believe the events taking place in the parking lot.

Through the giant glass windows that made up the front entrance of the club, Mason was horrified at what he was seeing. The club members and employees that had left only moments before were being run down and attacked by these savages that seemingly came out of nowhere. People were running, falling, and literally being torn apart by these things.

One of heavier men who only ten minutes before walked out the front door in a hurry to get to his car and vacate the area was now in a flat out sprint back toward the facility. He missed the step up onto the curb, went down hard, and slid face first into the glass entrance. The closed doors acted as a dead end for this man as three of those things were on him in seconds.

Mason's first reaction was to head toward the door and offer some sort of help, although the huge glass wall thirty feet in front of him was offering the only line of protection for him at this point. What kind of help was he going to offer anyway? These things seemed to be much stronger and looked as if they were literally feeding on anyone who came into their line of sight.

He figured there must be at least a hundred of them outside. While trying to come up with an escape plan, Mason knelt behind the desk not only to get out of sight, but also to block his view of the atrocious scene that lay before him. He had seen enough and needed to clear his head.

Mason needed to get to April and Justin; if her father was right, it had to be sooner rather than later. He looked back around the side of the desk and the focus of the mob had moved away from the parking lot and grown closer to the building.

There had to be a dozen or so bodies pressed up against the glass while being torn apart.

He knew Tom kept a revolver in the locked cabinet under his desk. Mason got to his feet and made a break for the office. This time the crowd saw him and started pounding against the glass like a riot at a heavy metal concert. Mason slid into the office and behind the desk. "Not good!" He noticed the drawer open and the gun missing. Tom must have grabbed it on his way out. The pounding continued to escalate until there was a gigantic crash and Mason knew they were now inside.

Knowing his only option was to run, Mason grabbed his bag from the floor and noticed the revolver just outside the office. It must have fallen out of Tom's bag as he left in such a hurry.

Mason could hear the pounding footsteps getting closer as he grabbed the gun and continued to sprint toward the staircase at the back of the building that led to the roof. There was no other way out. Mason feared he would be trapped inside and eaten alive.

As he reached the stairs, the horde was only yards away from him and closing in fast. Mason refused to look back as he knew that would slow him down. As he pushed himself up the stairs with his legs he also used the handrail to pull himself toward the top in an attempt to move that much faster. Mason feared he would trip or miss a step and that would be it.

He didn't want to die here on this staircase. As he reached the top, he prayed the exit wasn't locked. He looked back and was pleased when he realized he had put some distance between himself and the deranged crowd. As he glanced over his shoulder before reaching the door, it looked as if those things were falling over each other to get up the stairs first.

Thankfully, the door to the roof was unlocked. As he burst through the door and onto the rooftop, Mason was momentarily blinded as the sun had broken through the clouds and was now drying what little rain had fallen.

As his sight became clear again, he twisted from side to side taking it all in. Every area, as far as the eye could see looked like a war zone. There were fires covering large parts of the city, car alarms sounding every few seconds, and screams of terror filling what little silence there was.

"What is this?" he said aloud.

Mason remembered the vacant furniture store to the right had closed six months ago and might still be untouched as he couldn't see any turmoil coming from that direction.

As the crowd reached the door to the roof, Mason put his head down and sprinted in the direction of the vacant store.

"This may have been a terrible idea."

The distance he needed to jump now appeared much farther than he remembered. He knew if he didn't clear the large space between the two buildings that he would fall the thirty plus feet to the ground below and at the very least break his legs and become food for these monsters.

With only twenty feet before the edge and

adrenaline coursing through every ounce of his body, he could actually feel their footsteps coming from behind.

Mason dug in to increase his speed and with his last step he launched himself over the gap.

4

April tossed the phone on the bed, grabbed her shoes, and ran down the stairs before heading to the front door and making sure it was unlocked. She knew from looking out the window that the walkway on the left side of the house was clear and a direct line to the entrance of the school. She decided to go out the back door and walk over instead of taking the car as there was no chance of driving into the parking lot anytime in the next few hours.

Walking through the yard and out the side gate, April looked back and saw the neighbors gathered in the street, obviously discussing the events of the day. They motioned for her to come over and she yelled back in their direction, "I'll be back in a few minutes." She didn't want any company for her trip to the school and back since they'd slow her down.

The area outside the school looked intimidating to April. She pushed ahead and ran across the two lanes of traffic that led to the school. She watched as angry parents screamed all sorts of obscenities at one another from their halted vehicles. Out of frustration, one man even got out and kicked the door of the car in front of him. These people were not going anywhere and April was glad she had decided to walk.

A large group formed outside the entrance to the school where teachers and staff members were trying to account for each student leaving. A few of the parents attempted to exit the area without checking their children out and were met with a stern faculty member guiding them back toward the office. One overly aggressive mother refused to bend to their demands and hurried her twins into the car, only to be blocked by the biggest teacher April had ever seen. This is not helping to speed up the process, she thought.

April realized that if she followed their rules, she wouldn't get to see her son for at least an hour and that wasn't going to work. She stopped for a moment, looked around, and noticed the left side of the school where students were exiting the rear of the gym to the field. Since the entire mob was focused on the entrance, she decided to head in the direction of the escaping students.

As she walked briskly, trying to be inconspicuous, April pulled her cell phone out of her pocket and sent a text to Justin. Where are you? I'm coming around the back of the school through the gym. April continued to get closer to the rear entrance, and upon looking back found to her delight that she had gone unnoticed. Justin's text came through just as quick. I'm at the door to the library. The office is a nightmare.

April reached the entrance to the rear of the gym as the few inventive kids continued to pour out. One of them looked over at her as they passed in the doorway.

"Hey lady, I wouldn't go in there; it's a ZOO!"

"Yeah... You should see the front."

April fired off a reply to Justin as she made her way across the gym floor. Meet me in front of Mrs. Wood's classroom and we will leave from there.

She knew the classrooms and halls would be nearly empty, as all the students were pushing toward the front entrance and there would be no chance of getting through that crowd anytime soon.

Justin hopped down from the table he was sitting on, slung his backpack over his shoulder, and started toward the hall that led to his math class.

The office admin, without even looking up, yelled at him through the crowd. "Excuse me Justin, where do you think you're going?" Thinking quickly he answered, "I dropped my math book just around the corner. I'll be right back." She seemed to buy his excuse as she continued whatever it was she was doing on her computer and waved him on.

Justin turned the corner and, once out of her view, ran down the hall toward his math class, noticing he was the only one in this wing of the school.

Making her way out of the gym and into the long hallway that led past the locker rooms and into the rest of the school, April remembered Mrs. Wood's class being down the third hall.

She thought back to the last time she was this deep inside the school and figured it was last year's open house where she learned Justin was in the top five percent of students in the district academically. Justin was the type of student that thrived on doing well, although he would never tell a soul as he hated the attention it brought. Justin would rather that no one knew just how brilliant he really was. He liked the friends he had and feared he would be labeled as a freak for being so smart.

April was happy to discover that her memory served her right and she had chosen the right hallway. As soon as she rounded the corner she could see Justin down at the end of the hall sitting on a folding chair, peering down at his phone. She waited until she was a little closer and didn't have to yell, so they wouldn't alert anyone that they were here before she said, "Hey, you ready to get out of here?"

Justin looked up. "Mom!"

April immediately ran over to Justin, threw her arms around him and said, "Let's go."

"Uh Mom... Some of my friends are texting me that people are getting really hurt down at the front of the school."

"I don't doubt it; there must be a few thousand people out there," April replied.

"No, they said people are REALLY hurting each

other; they said some people may have even been killed."

"I'm sure nothing like that has happened, but I'll bet most of the people stuck out in that mess wish they hadn't all tried to come at the same time."

"Look at the photo Billy just sent me."

Justin turned his phone so April could see the image. She almost let out a shriek as the horror of what she saw startled her. It was a blurry image although she could tell it was one man ripping the flesh from another man's neck with his bare hands.

She kept her composure so she wouldn't frighten Justin. "Come on, you know he's playing with you. I'm sure that is a photoshopped picture from the internet."

"Mom, I don't think it is; we can't get online here at school, it's blocked."

"I'm sure there some sort of an explanation..."

As April was trying to calm Justin, they heard a low rumble that built into what sounded like a stampede heading in their direction. Justin looked at April just as a massive crowd rounded the corner toward them.

It appeared they were being chased, although it wasn't quite apparent what they were running from until a few grimy, disheveled, homeless looking men took down the school's security staff at the rear of the crowd, even after being shot more than once.

These men were covered in blood and

seemingly on a mission to destroy anything they came into contact with. They literally pulled the three security guards apart limb by limb until there was nothing left of them. They then turned their focus on the rest of the crowd.

As they grew closer, Justin froze in place. April grabbed his hand and pulled him backward into the classroom, knocking them both to the floor.

Justin scrambled to get to his feet and looked at his mother in horror.

"Mom, what are those things?"

5

As he soared over the void, Mason felt fortunate that the roof of the vacant furniture store was a good five feet below that of the gym. If the gap between the two rooflines had been any more than what Mason estimated at fifteen feet, he surely would have ended up on the ground below.

Surveying the spot where was he was to land and the rest of the rooftop, Mason noticed one of the things he had been running from at the far edge, seemingly looking for a way off. Mason wasn't much concerned as once he touched down, he figured they would still be a good sixty feet apart. That would give him at least a few seconds to get his wits about him before he was challenged.

Landing hard on his feet, then immediately to his knees, and finally falling forward onto his left side, Mason slid across the damp rooftop. Once he came to a stop, Mason jumped to his feet and was amazed to find he had only acquired a few scrapes, other than that he was good to go.

Mason watched as many of these things followed him over the edge, but without jumping, so they all ended up at the bottom of the alley between the two buildings, one on top of another. Mason was stunned when many of them just stood and walked back toward the crowd at the front of the building.

Looking back across the roof he just landed on, Mason realized that he had hardly even been noticed by his new adversary. Only the noise of him crashing down caused it to slowly turn in Mason's direction.

Mason stared at this thing and it stared back, in the same way a bull does just before it runs down the bullfighter. He didn't seem to be interested in Mason, but more curious at why he was here; he even cocked his head to the left.

Most of the other freaks Mason had seen today were fairly normal looking, with the exception of their eyes. They didn't seem to focus on any one thing and they didn't look you in the face. They gave the impression that they were on a mission to destroy any human in their path and lost all concern for their own safety.

Standing a mere fifty feet from this creature, Mason yelled the only thing he could think of.

"Why?"

It straightened its head and started toward Mason. As it approached Mason knew something was different about this one. It didn't move half as fast as the others and it was in much worse condition, possibly hurt.

As it got closer Mason still didn't feel

threatened. He began to notice the skin on its face and arms was torn off in places and was hanging by little shards in others. The clothes it had on weren't in any better shape and looked as if they had gone through a wood chipper just before it got dressed.

Twenty feet away and getting closer, Mason realized that its ankle was snapped in two and its foot was being dragged. He slid off his backpack, set it on the ground to his right, and withdrew the revolver.

This thing was bigger than Mason had initially accounted for and he began to get nervous, even though it wasn't moving very quickly. Mason retreated to the edge of the roof with his back to the chasm. He changed his mind about the gun and slid it into his waistband, realizing that if he squeezed off a shot, every one of those things would be drawn to him immediately.

With only two paces left between them, Mason braced his rear foot against the drain pipe at the edge of the building and crouched into a defensive position. Mouth open, the creature lunged at him as Mason grabbed its forearm and pulled it to the ground. It didn't seem to fight being pulled down; its only focus appeared to be Mason's flesh.

As he held it down and dragged it to the edge, it began twisting and turning its neck almost to the point of dislocation, the whole time snapping at Mason's arm and face. Once he had it on its back and close enough, Mason released his grip, stepped back and kicked it over the side to the ground below.

It smashed into the asphalt and was deformed even more from the impact. Much to Mason's astonishment, it slowly righted itself, stood and began heading toward the rear of the building, although at a much slower rate than before.

Shaking his head he muttered, "What the hell has happened?"

Mason reached for the gun that had fallen while he had his hands full with that thing. He walked a few steps further, grabbing the backpack and heading toward the opposite end of the building.

When he reached the northeast corner, Mason surveyed the end of the parking lot furthest from the gym and noticed only a few of those things slowing roaming the area. From his vantage point, he could see that the side of town nearest Justin's school and his former home appeared untouched.

It was only two miles away and he could run there if he had to, although his car was a much faster and safer option. April and Justin needed him and there was no time to spare.

He just needed to get past the growing horde that still occupied the part of the lot where he was parked. If the scene that played out earlier in the day were any indication of what he was up against, this may be the last challenge he would ever face.

6

"Justin... JUSTIN!"

April was now shouting at him. She looked toward the door and asked, "How do you lock it?" She shook Justin, who appeared to be in a state of shock. He just stared out the door as horrified classmates and school staff ran past and flooded into other classrooms.

April grabbed a textbook from his backpack and slammed it on the desk next to her making a loud crashing sound and waking Justin from his trance. "Mom, are we going to die?"

"NO, but I need to know how to lock the door." April tried to reassure Justin, although she wasn't so sure they would make it out.

"It only locks from the outside and you need a key."

April looked around and grabbed the desk next to her. "Let's push some of these against the door and maybe slow them down."

"What about my friends and the teachers? We

can't lock them out."

"So far no one has tried to get in; they all look like they are more interested in going down that other hall."

They quickly slid five desks in front of the door and they piled another six on top. They figured that if it didn't stop whatever those things were from getting in, it would at least slow them down enough to give them a few minutes head start in getting as far away from here as possible.

Looking toward the rear of the classroom, April asked, "Where does that door go, can we get to the gym from there?"

"Yeah, but we have to go past the hall that those things were in."

April thought about it for a moment. "Ok, let's go."

The pair headed for the rear door, only to find it was locked. Justin ran back to the teacher's desk and grabbed the stapler. He hurried back to the door and made short work of the lock. They could still hear the muted cries for help and the terrible screaming coming from the south end of the school where most of the destruction appeared to be taking place.

Through the door there appeared a long hallway with only one outlet to the left. "Where does that go?" April asked.

"After the bend, it splits and goes to the front office and the other side goes to the hallway that goes to the band room and the gym."

April paused for a moment, trying to gather the

courage she would need to move forward. More than anything right now, April needed to be strong for her son. She would give her last dying breath for him if necessary. April was prepared to give herself to those things if it meant Justin would go free. She didn't want these thoughts to slow her down or to frighten her to the point of not being able to act when he needed her to be strong.

She decided to let the fear in and have it wash over her. April purposely let it control her and completely paralyze her with terror for a moment and from then on she would not give in to it. She had a job to do and fear would not slow her down another second.

April looked Justin in the eyes. "Let's go. I want you to stay very close to me and if you spot one of those things or need to tell me something, I want you to tug on my shirt and then only in whispers. We are going to be silent until we get out of school. I do not want any of those things finding us. Are you good?"

"Yeah... But..."

"But what?" April said.

"I have to pee."

"You're going to have to hold it; I don't plan on being in this school more than a few minutes. You can pee at home."

April grabbed Justin by the hand and pulled him down the lengthy hallway. Picking up speed, they moved faster with each passing second, although not into a full run, as this would create too much noise.

They finally reached the split that led to the

gym. They could still hear the terror going on, although it appeared to moving away from them.

Justin whispered to his mother and pointed. "It's just past that pillar on the right."

"Alright, stay close."

April and Justin made their way down the last of the corridor before reaching the midpoint of the school that housed the computer lab and the janitor's office, both of which had seen better days. The computer lab had a small fire burning that appeared to be extinguishing itself. The door to the janitor's office was completely ripped from its hinges and a body lay motionless just inside.

Tiptoeing past the two rooms, they looked back and could see that the front half of the school had taken the same level of abuse. Books, backpacks, and lunch bags were everywhere. There were a few more bodies near the entrance and the front doors were blown out; glass littered the entire area.

Looking back as they continued toward the gym, they could partially see into the teachers' lounge. You could tell they had fought to keep those things out and lost the battle. Four bodies were left behind.

April looked at Justin again and she could tell the fear was getting the best of him. "Slow down your breathing and just give me a few minutes. We will be safe and at home before you know it."

They started to walk slowly and she looked back again. "Your dad is meeting us at home; everything is going to be fine. WE are going to be fine."

They hurried forward again, across the open area into the hall leading to the gym. Justin looked left and noticed one of those things hunched over the assistant principal, who was no longer moving. Justin nearly screamed when he saw this and April covered his mouth.

It was too late—the thing looked up from its prey and found its next target.

7

Making his way back over to the ladder attached to the side of the building, Mason was pleased when he looked down and none of those things occupied the area below. He tightened the slings of the backpack around his shoulders and wrapped his right leg around to meet the fourth rung.

Halfway down the ladder, Mason noticed the same character he had thrown off the opposite end of the building only minutes before rounding the corner at the rear of the building to his left. He noticed it was moving even slower than it had before and that he was in no danger of it reaching him before he exited the ladder.

"Hey Fred," he said aloud, mocking his new slowly moving friend, knowing it posed him no threat at this point. Mason almost felt bad for him until he remembered that Fred tried to eat him not even five minutes before. Mason thought of jumping down, running over and smashing Fred's skull against the side of the furniture store. He knew better than to waste his time since he wasn't out of danger just yet.

Mason turned his attention back toward the front corner of the building. It appeared quiet with none of those things anywhere in sight. With only a few rungs left, Mason leapt to the ground below and waved goodbye to his dear friend Fred. "It's been nice buddy, although I got to go and I don't think you're gonna be able to keep up. I hate long goodbyes so..." Mason made himself laugh just a little as he turned to run.

Coming to the corner that led to the storefront, Mason looked out over the lot and found his car. It was much further than he remembered, probably because he was checking texts as he walked into the gym that afternoon. There appeared to be less of those things roaming the lot than earlier and they now seemed to be moving in packs of ten to twenty.

They were also moving slower than before, although he didn't want to get caught between two of these herds and end up having them pull him apart from both ends.

There were still people trying to escape, Mason counted at least a half dozen or so. Some were hiding behind trees and planters, while others continued to run, trying to reach their cars with enough time to get inside and get moving before the crowds converged on them.

A lump grew in Mason's throat as he noticed his friend Tom hiding behind one of the big palm trees only thirty feet from his car. He had to help Tom and somehow distract those things without bringing them to him.

Mason pulled off the backpack and withdrew the revolver. He hoped to be able to hit at least a couple of those things and clear a path for the two of them to get the hell out of there. As Mason searched for a target, he suddenly had a completely different idea.

Mason lowered the gun and fired off a round. A mere millisecond later, the metal dumpster at the far end of the lot exploded in a deafening roar that sent shockwaves in every direction, confusing everyone, including the hordes. This caused those things to split off, moving in different directions, going after no one in particular.

Looking back and noticing Fred still wasn't much closer and had now fallen to the ground, Mason shook his head, stood, and started toward his car. "Poor guy never had a chance." Most of the vile creatures walking the lot hadn't noticed him yet as he moved quickly and quietly. Mason moved from tree to tree trying to avoid being spotted and it almost looked as if he may make it to his car unharmed.

When he was a little more than halfway, Tom finally saw him and, making eye contact, started waving him away. Much to his dismay, at this point Mason also had the attention of eight to ten of the creatures and more were on to him with every second that passed.

He knew he didn't have enough ammo for all that were coming for him. Mason quickened his pace and was now almost sprinting. He looked back and saw that Tom had the same idea and was also making a break for his car, although he had gained the attention of many more of those things than Mason had.

Just feet from his car, Mason hit the button on his alarm key unlocking the doors. He didn't want to look back as he heard the footsteps getting closer. He knew he only had one shot at this and reached out, opened the door and slid into the driver's seat all in one motion. Those things must have been close because they were on the car only seconds after Mason turned the key, starting the engine.

Looking for an easy exit, Mason noticed Tom had dropped his keys only feet from his car and was bent over trying to pick them off the ground when three of them converged on him.

Tom stood from a kneeling position, sending two of the creatures reeling backward and to the ground. The last one Tom pulled off his back and threw it to the ground. Tom stood over the one nearest him and stomped on its face. The two that Tom had sent flying backward were getting to their feet, and due to all the commotion, Mason counted no less than seven additional creatures headed in Tom's direction.

Mason put the car in gear, pushed the pedal to the floor and pointed the car in the direction of the crowd gathering near Tom. Tom looked up in disbelief as Mason bore down on the crowd. There were so many of them now it was hard to even tell Tom from the rest of the crowd. Mason hit one of them, almost tearing its body in half and when he applied the brakes he took out another two or three as the car slid sideways to a stop directly in front of Tom.

Trying to get his bearings after the collision with the crowd, Mason noticed his friend being pulled to the ground by a few of those things that still remained upright. Tom went down hard, hitting the back of his head on the asphalt in the process.

His instinct was to put the car back in drive and get the hell out of there, although he knew he couldn't leave Tom to die here surrounded by these things. Mason slowly lowered the passenger window and he stuck his head out. He couldn't believe what he saw. Tom was lying on the ground just feet from the car, encircled by those things, passed out.

With nothing to lose and time running out, Mason shouted to him, "TOM!" and once again, "TOM, WAKE UP DAMN IT!"

Tom's faced twitched and his body shook, finally trying to open his eyes.

Mason was relieved to see that Tom was beginning to wake, although upon looking around his joy instantly turned to fear as many of those things also started to rise. He knew his friend wouldn't make it into the car on his own.

Mason had to get out and rescue him.

8

As the creature focused his gaze on the two of them, April leaned into Justin and whispered in his ear.

"Run," she said softly as not to alert any more of those things as to their whereabouts. This time Justin didn't hesitate and he made a beeline for the double doors that led into the gym. As they approached the midway point, he looked back to see his mother only a step behind. Justin was impressed by the fact that his mother was able to stay that close as he was in a full-out sprint.

This happy moment was soon overshadowed when he realized that the thing was not more than ten steps behind them. Justin was also dismayed when he turned to look back a second time and saw that they had picked up three additional enemies who were practically fighting each other to get to them first.

As they approached the door, Justin threw it open and stood aside to give his mother room to get by. When April reached the threshold, one of those things caught them and now had her by the upper arm. The trailing three all ran straight into the first creature, in turn pushing April through the door as the three of them scrambled to grab onto anything they could.

Justin pulled his mother from one end as two of those things fought each other for the rights to devour April. Not quite able to coordinate pulling her toward them and sinking their teeth into her at the same time, Justin was somewhat able to get the upper hand.

April was fighting just as hard to shake them free, and at the same time screaming at the top of her lungs. She thought about the promise she made herself about not letting the fear in and pulled even harder.

The creature closest to her pulled her closer and brought its head down, its mouth opening as April struggled again. This time it landed a bite; luckily for her, it only connected with her sleeve and tore it right off.

"Mom, let them have your shirt."

As April wiggled free of her sweatshirt, Justin pulled at just the right time, sending the last two creatures staggering backward. Justin pulled again and April shot forward with only one arm left to get free of.

Justin's grip started to fail from this seemingly endless battle of deranged tug-of-war.

"I won't let go," he told his mother.

"You better not!"

Justin saw that his mother had cleared the entrance to the gym and as the thing came in for another bite, he pulled her one last time with everything he had left and kicked the door at the same time with his left foot. The door caught the thing on the side of the head and it released its grip on her. Justin and April both fell backwards into the empty gym as the creature moved to stand.

Justin rushed back over to the door, not quite knowing what to expect. He pushed the door from the inside and this time he heard bones cracking. He had become incensed with these things for what he and his mother were being put through.

Again he slammed the door, and again. He continued to open and close the door until its head was smashed in two and the top part of the skull fell at Justin's feet.

The other two were still trying to climb over the corpse which blocked the doorway in a bloody heap when Justin slammed the door one last time catching one of the creature's hands in the door and obliterating it.

Justin turned to his mother, reached out his hand to help her stand and said "Let's go."

April stood, and wiped a few drops of blood off Justin's face. "Are you OK?"

"I am now... we have to get out of here Mom; do you think they are all locked inside?"

"I guess we are going to find out," April said as they started toward the exit.

As the approached the doors leading to the outside, they could hear scratching and pounding at the door.

They looked at one another and Justin was the first to speak. "That's not good," he said.

"No, it's not... is there any other way out of this gym?"

"Only back through the school. Wait a second," Justin said as he jogged over to the door next to the athletic director's office.

"Where are you going?"

"Hold on mom. Give me a minute; I have a plan."

Justin disappeared into the room and April heard lots of clanking and clattering just as he emerged carrying three items, a baseball bat, glove, and hockey stick.

"There's no time for this Justin, we need a plan to get home."

"Mom, this IS our plan."

9

Reacting without a plan in mind, Mason flung the driver's door open, stepped out and was instantly being clawed at from below by the creatures that had taken the brunt of the hit from the car. He stepped back and away from them, looking around for something to use to keep them off of him.

Mason had thoughts of being clawed and bitten to death by these things surrounding him and Tom. He thought of how it would feel to have his skin ripped from his body while watching it happen and wondered how long it would take to finally lose consciousness and slip to the other side. That isn't going to happen, he thought, as another one of them grabbed at his leg, trying to bring him down, not unlike a cheetah trying to pull down a gazelle for its next meal.

Looking in through the back window of his car, he spotted what would be his way out of this parking lot of hell. As the creatures fought to get to their feet, Mason kicked free from yet another one and pulled open the back door of the car.

With one motion, Mason reached into the backseat, withdrew a ten pound kettlebell and swung it backward, making contact with another one of them attacking from behind. Striking it right in the middle of the face, the impact was so violent that it lifted the thing off its feet and sent it flying more than five feet until it came to rest flat on its back. The noise of metal to bone sent a shiver up Mason's spine. It sounded like a hammer hitting a hardboiled egg. He felt the recoil of bones being smashed to pieces as tiny fragments of blood and flesh sprayed against his arms and back.

Mason turned to face the horde. Realizing the majority of them had taken the easy route and rounded the car after Tom, he took two steps and slid over the hood of the car and began to take swing after swing at the now diminishing crowd surrounding his friend.

Most of the other hungry monsters hadn't even looked back to notice Mason taking them apart one by one. As they grew closer to their prey, so did their single-minded focus.

Mason suddenly realized these things seemed to go down for good if he smashed their heads severely enough. That was the only sign of hope he needed. Instead of battering them in the chest, arms, or shoulders, Mason began to focus his aim on their heads. He also picked up the force with which he swung his newfound weapon.

He was nearly within arm's reach of his friend when the shouting for help turned to screams of agony. They had gotten ahold of Tom and there was nothing he could do at this point. He cursed at them, although they didn't even look up.

He was too late.

From where Mason stood, he could see them tearing the skin from his abdomen and upper thigh. Tom continued to fight as they tore at him. He punched and kicked them, although he had no chance as these things appeared unfazed by any of the blows he landed.

They shoved their faces down, pulling back scraps of flesh, and began devouring Tom. There were only two left, although the damage was apparent. They dug into his belly and shoved the bloody mess into their mouths. The heartbreaking screams began to taper off until they were fully muted, as in their last act of violence they began tearing and biting at his face and neck.

His eyes remained open, although Tom was now gone.

Mason struggle to understand how it happened so quickly and why he didn't react fast enough to beat these things off of his friend.

As the two began to struggle over what remained of Tom's body, Mason raised the kettlebell and swung it down on top of one of them with so much force that it instantly went limp. Its skull was split into two jagged pieces and a thick river of blood ran past Mason's shoe as hundreds of bone fragments littered the area.

Pieces also ricocheted off the one still hunched over Tom's lifeless body. It looked over to see what it was just as Mason swung from the side. This one fell back and to the side as its head became dislodged from its body.

Mason thought it was odd that, from the shoulders down, this thing appeared to be a slightly disheveled businessman dressed to impress. The only indicator that something wasn't quite right here was that its head lay fifteen feet behind it.

With the brain stem still attached and the obvious trauma that grotesquely marked its face, it looked more like a science experiment gone wrong than something that was once human.

Mason knelt at the passenger door of his car, weeping for what seemed an eternity. Bruised and bloody, he knew what he had just witnessed would change him forever. He had just seen his good friend being murdered by whatever these things were. He wasn't going to let this happen to anyone else he cared about. He couldn't.

Coming out of the fog that trapped him in sorrow for the last few minutes, Mason realized he needed to snap out of it and get to April and Justin before this evil fell upon them. Looking out over the lot, he saw a new group of those things headed his way.

Brushing the fleshy fragments from his clothes, Mason moved back to the other side of the car, tossed the kettlebell in the back seat and shut the door.

Sliding into the driver's seat, he put the car in drive and paused for a moment. He needed a clear route back to the house if he was going to make it in time, and knew that all of the main streets would probably be a nightmare to get through.

As he departed the lot, Mason maneuvered around the discarded shards of flesh and the growing crowds at the north end of the lot. Looking in the rearview mirror, he noticed the horde turned in his direction in the hopes of yet another meal.

Pulling out onto the street, Mason mentally went through his route back to the house and intended to run down anything that got in his way.

10

Looking at him sideways, April wasn't quite sure what the sporting equipment had to do with them getting out of this gym alive, although she thought the bat would be a good start.

"Are you going to let me in on this plan of yours or do I have to guess?"

"Mom, take this hockey stick and glove."

"OK?"

"I am going to use the bat to take as many of those things out as possible and I want you to use the stick to keep them away. If they get too close, push them back with the stick. If possible knock them down; they don't seem to get back up too fast."

She wasn't quite sure this would work, although they had no other plan; and from the sounds of it, the crowd outside the door was growing.

"Justin, how are we going to get the door open?"

"It doesn't sound like they are pushing up

against it, so we may be able to surprise them and knock over the first few of them."

"What's this glove for?"

"That's in case they get REALLY close. Shove it against their faces; it will take them forever to chew through it."

Justin wasn't sure any of this would work. He was trying to sound confident so his mother would have enough faith in the plan to pull off what she needed to do.

"Mom?"

"Yeah?"

"Is Dad really coming or are you just saying that?"

"I talked to him just a little while ago and he was on his way home."

"Our home?"

"Yep."

"Do you think he is OK?"

"You know your Dad, even if he wasn't you'd never know."

"Alright Mom, let's go... and please stay by me."

"YES SIR," April said with a smile.

Justin walked toward the door and depressed the panic bar without pushing the door open just yet.

He whispered to his mother, "On three push as hard as you can. One... Two...THREE!"

As they pushed both sides of the exit door outward, they felt some resistance, although not as much as they were expecting, and only a few of those things were near the doorway. The majority of them littered the field between them and their home. The fifty yards between the gym and the outer fence wouldn't normally be anything other than a short jog; however, today was a different story.

The problem was getting to the fence and over it unharmed; once they reached the other side, they would be free. It seemed like these things hadn't figured out how to climb because the street on the other side was clear of all creatures. Justin looked around for the easiest path and decided they needed to go in a straight line since no other ideal route existed.

Justin took the lead and swung at anything that came near. He noticed that these things could take an incredible amount of pain and still keep coming. Striking them in the legs appeared to work pretty well as it slowed most of them down to a crawl almost instantly.

The more Justin went on the offensive, the less fear he felt. He imagined himself in control and these things only doing what he would allow. As they progressed forward, Justin would slide four or five steps ahead, clear the way, and come back for April as she made sure that none of them snuck up from behind.

About the time they reached the midway point, most of the creatures near the field had turned their attention to the two of them and Justin's arms started to fatigue.

Pointing in the direction of the growing horde, Justin motioned to April.

"Mom, we need to get to the fence quick. I can't

keep swinging this all day. Let's run!"

Justin waited for his mother to acknowledge his request and as she began to run ahead, he followed closely. As they ran, April dropped the stick and glove and Justin almost tripped over them. He also dropped the bat and instead picked up the hockey stick, figuring it would be more useful once they reached the gate.

As he stood again after grabbing the stick and began to run, he caught April quickly. With just a step between them April stepped in a gopher hole and went down hard, causing Justin in turn to tumble over her.

At least ten of those things were closing in on them from the rear as they stood to continue. April grabbed at her ankle and winced in pain. With only fifteen yards to go, Justin wrapped his mother's arm around his shoulder and pulled her alongside him without saying a word.

Justin had only passed her in height and weight within the last year and was growing rapidly ever since. He was bigger than most kids three years his senior and had the strength to match. Being carried by her son seemed odd as she thought back to when he was a child and could never have imagined a day when she would have needed him for this. She recently gave in to the fact that he would take after his father since his side of the family had all the height.

With only a few yards to go, they were finally caught by two of those things. Justin shoved April forward toward the fence as he stayed back to fight. He now wished more than anything that he had kept the bat.

"GET OVER THAT FENCE!" Justin yelled at his mother as he moved from side to side, pulling free from the bigger of the two creatures.

April struggled to climb the six foot chain-link fence with only one good leg. Her hands were bloody and she felt as if she didn't have the strength to get over. She pulled with everything inside her and used her other foot as an anchor.

Justin saw a softball sized stone lying next to an anthill just to his right. As he broke free once again, he picked up the stone before turning to see April nearing the top of the fence. Justin lifted the stone overhead and brought it down hard on the smaller of the two. Blood shot across his face and ran down his shirt.

As he turned the stone on the larger one, it lunged at him and knocked him to the ground, landing directly on top of him. Justin fell hard and felt the unforgiving earth beneath him. He pushed away and the thing on top of him growled like a hungry lion about to consume its prey.

With only eighteen inches separating their faces, Justin instantly became nauseous looking at the shredded, decaying flesh hanging from its mouth and neck. Its eyes were covered with a milky white substance and Justin couldn't understand how it was able to see.

It came in again, mouth wide open, straining to get to Justin's neck as he rolled to the side and avoided the creature's teeth. Justin had never been so terrified and was reacting more out of fear than anything else. He noticed April starting back over the fence toward him.

"NO!"

April stopped as Justin managed to slide his way out from under his attacker and grabbed the weapon he dropped moments before. From a seated position he swung, but because the stone was wet with blood, it only grazed his target and fell to the ground.

Enraged, Justin leapt on top of this behemoth and grabbed it by both sides of the head. He slid to the right and brought the creature's head down numerous times on top of the rock that lay beneath it until the thing stopped struggling and its skull was completely obliterated.

Justin stood and looked at April. She didn't say a word and just started to cry. Justin wiped his hands and arms on his pants and walked to the fence.

He took one final look back and with no other threats anywhere nearby, he climbed the fence and helped his mother to the other side.

April wrapped her arm around Justin's neck once again as she continued to quietly cry. Heads hung low, they both headed toward the house.

11

His plan was almost instantly ruined as Mason looked down the street that was the most direct route home and noticed a jagged line of cars stalled and dozens of those things walking about.

Slowing the car to a crawl, he saw an opening a hundred yards down on the right that led to the parking lot of a condominium tract. He thought he would be able to get through there quickly and pick up Ranch Boulevard.

Normally, the Alpine Trail condos were pretty empty at this time of day since most tenants worked in the city and were gone during the typical nine to five. Mason used this shortcut many times when he was late meeting a client at the gym. From what he had seen this morning, if people weren't around, neither were those creatures... whatever they were.

After reversing the car just enough to turn down the street, he pushed forward, trying to move slowly enough not to create much noise and alert them as they rummaged through the vehicles farther down the road. Before he was halfway to the driveway of the condos, they spotted him heading their way.

It was strange to Mason that some of these things moved fairly quickly and seemed to be almost normal, with the exception of their eyes being glossed over. They appeared unable to focus on anything. They didn't even move their eyes. If a noise was made, they would move their entire head in the direction of the sound, almost as if they had a stiff neck.

The others that moved more slowly looked as if they had literally been hit by a car or something bigger. He thought that whatever was affecting them made them deteriorate rather quickly until they reached a point where they actually looked like death and weren't able to move much faster than a slow walk.

Weaving in and out of the slow moving creatures, Mason reached the condo entrance and was greeted by two of them slowly moving toward the front of his car. Without thinking, he punched the gas pedal and turned to the left side of the entrance, grazing one of them. The other grabbed onto the rear bumper and was dragged for a minute or so until it eventually slid off.

The only thing that remained in the parking lot was a few cars still sitting in their little stalls under the overhangs that protected them from the elements. His path was clear all the way to the end of the complex and he only needed to turn right at the end of the drive and then left out onto Ranch

Blvd.

After putting some distance between himself and his attackers, Mason rounded the corner to the right and slammed on the brakes. A man leapt over the hood of the car and one of those things following close behind him ran straight into the side of Mason's car, knocking the side mirror to the ground.

Mason looked out the window and watched as it slid across the side of the car and went down hard. Blood now covered half of the front passenger window. He quickly pulled out into the street and tried to catch up to this man who was still running from his attacker, unaware that he was no longer in danger.

Looking in the rearview mirror, Mason could see the thing that had just abused the side of his car walking out into the middle of the street and heading his way. He needed to get to the man running ahead of him before that thing did, without making a huge production of it.

As Mason pulled the car alongside the man, he was impressed with his stamina. The man nearly jumped out of his shoes as he realized there was something next to him. He looked relieved and slowed to a jog as he looked over his shoulder and noticed that he had put a safe distance between him and his pursuer.

Mason lowered the passenger window as blood and scraps of flesh rolled off the car and a few pieces dropped into the seat next to him.

"Hey buddy, you need a lift?" Mason said with a smile.

"That was my father-in-law!"

"What?"

"That Feeder, it was my father-in-law."

Mason looked confused. "That what?"

"FEEDER! Where have you been? It's all over the news, that's what they're calling them."

"Get in," Mason said as he pushed the door open.

The man readily got in the car, looking hysterical. He was a middle-aged, professional looking gentleman. From the cut of his hair to the dry cleaned shirt he was wearing, Mason figured he was some sort of executive. He trained guys like this all the time. He was obviously in good shape as evidenced by how he hopped over the car and sprinted down the street at a pace that would make any college-level track athlete blush.

As his new passenger closed the door, Mason drove on again.

"Hey, I'm Mason," he said as he held out his disgusting hand.

"REALLY glad to meet you, I'm William." The passenger looked down at Mason's bloody offering and shook it all the same.

"William, you're telling me that thing chasing you was your father-in-law?"

"Yes until about fifteen minutes ago."

"Huh?"

"I live close by and my wife sent me over to check on her parents, so I decided to just walk over since they cleared Ranch Boulevard."

"Cleared it, who cleared it?"

"The Police, you haven't been near a computer, have you?"

"No, I was at work when this all came down a few hours ago and we saw a few news reports and that's it."

"It's all over the internet. They're calling them Feeders and they don't stay dead unless you shoot them in the head or smash their skulls in. They're saying it has something to do with severing the brain from the rest of the body."

Mason was trying to take this all in. "Ok how did your father-in-law end up chasing you?"

"I walked up to his condo and he was already gone and a Feeder was hunched over him. I smashed its head in with an axe I brought from home and it got stuck. I sat there for a moment trying to figure out what I was going to tell my wife when I got back home and he stood up."

"Your father-in-law?"

"Yes sir."

"What about your mother-in-law?" Mason asked.

"I couldn't find her, she wasn't there."

Mason looked over at William, his head in his hands and was glad he decided to take the shortcut. "You said you live close. Can I drop you at home?"

"Sure, do you know where the Redstone Development is?"

"Yep, up here off of Morgan Road, correct?"

"Yeah, that's it. Mason, do you live around here?"

"I used to live just three blocks up in Elderbrook."

"Used to?"

"Yeah, my wife... uh... I mean... never mind... yeah, I live close."

Defeated and hungry, Mason rolled the car to a stop at the corner of Ranch and Morgan. They both looked out the front windshield in astonishment. There must have been fifty vehicles, one up against another facing all directions. There were even cars up on the sidewalk against the light poles and stop signs, although there was not a soul in sight.

Mason spoke first. "No chance we're driving through that mess. You cool walking it from here?"

"Sure, I don't see any of those things around."

As they exited the car, Mason grabbed the backpack, slung it over his shoulder, reached back in for both kettlebells this time, and shut the door.

Mason walked around the front of the car and handed one of them to William.

"You may need this."

12

Crossing the street that led back home, April and Justin were exhausted. Not knowing when the next attack would occur or where it would come from, they continuously checked each direction every few seconds. They reached the gated path as Justin slowed to let his mother rest against the wall. He leaned in, slowly opened the gate and looked further down the path that ended near his home.

There was no sign of any of those things and strangely enough no other people as well. Justin came back for April, again taking the brunt of her weight off the bad ankle.

"Justin, I think I can do it on my own. You must be really tired. Let's get you inside."

"Mom, I'm good and I don't have to pee anymore. I can help you. I'm still a kid and have tons of energy... remember?"

"You're a teen now and yes you have way more energy than me."

"Do you think dad is home yet?"

"I hope so."

Making their way alongside their home between the two eight foot block walls that lined the path, Justin stopped for a moment and held up his index finger, motioning for April to give him one second. He ran back down the path to shut the gate behind them, preventing any unwanted guest from entering the neighborhood.

The calm turn to chaos as soon as they reached their street. It seemed every neighbor on the entire block was trying to exit the area at the same time. Some were still packing up their cars in a state of panic and others were already heading down the street towards the exit of the community.

April tried to pull Justin along to get him to the house as he stood transfixed by the scene around him. April could feel her ankle starting to throb and wondered if something was broken or fractured. She assumed that cruising over to the local emergency room for x-rays was not going to be on her to-do list this evening.

"Hey neighbor!" they heard from behind.

This startled April to the point she would have jumped into the air if it wasn't for her bum leg. Justin, also surprised, swung around to see John, their middle-aged, overweight neighbor standing there with a shotgun slung over his shoulder.

"John, put that thing away, you're going to scare neighborhood kids."

"April, most of the families with kids are long gone and even if they were here, it may do some good to put a little fear into them."

"Where are Lucy and Max?" April asked.

"They left for her mother's place in Nevada about 10 minutes ago in the other car." Leaning in, John continued, "They say it's a safe zone and the military has set up barriers for miles around."

"Are you going?"

"Yeah, I was just putting the last of the things into my car and then I'm gonna head out... You?"

"Not sure yet, but with this traffic it doesn't look like anyone is getting outta here soon."

"Alright April, take care and try to leave soon. You don't want to be bringing up the rear."

"Thanks. See you soon John... Tell Lucy and Max we said hello."

John trotted off to his car, threw a few items into the rear hatch, and pulled out of the driveway to wait in line with the hundreds of others trying to make their way out of town.

April looked back at Justin, now sitting on the wall dividing the two yards. He was just staring into the mess that had become their neighborhood. She wanted to let him know that everything was going to be fine and to try to at least halfway mean it, although that's not what was bothering him.

Looking toward the driveway, Mason's car was noticeably missing.

"He'll be here. Your dad ALWAYS does what he says he's going to do."

"That's not it... what if those things got him? He's out there by himself."

"I'm sure he's fine. He's probably stuck in that mess of traffic. I'm sure he'll be here soon."

"Can we get in the car and go check? His work is just a few miles away."

"You want to try to get through that?" April said, pointing toward the street lined with cars.

"Well, can we sit out here for a few minutes and wait?"

"Sounds good, in the meantime why don't you just try texting your father?"

"OK!"

Justin sat on the wall texting away as April looked out over the area, praying that Mason was safe and that he would be there soon. She didn't think they could survive without him. She couldn't forgive herself for letting her father influence her life with Mason. She desperately wanted to see him again, wrap her arms around him, and tell him how much she loved him.

Mason had told her he fell in love with her the second he set eyes on her, even though she barely knew he existed. They had worked together and even though it wasn't the greatest job, he quit so she wouldn't have any excuse not to date him. It was his calm demeanor and eagerness to seek out new and exciting ways to better himself that had drawn her to him and also what eventually tore them apart.

He could never stand still, always wanting to do things that challenged him, both mentally and physically. He was never the nine to five type of guy and this often made April uneasy due to her conventional upbringing. She wanted to settle down and ease into a daily routine of schedules and time lines… and that made Mason feel nauseous.

Their two personalities had worked well together for many years until her father, the military man that he was, started to inject his point of view at every opportunity. Mason eventually got fed up and began to resent April for not standing up for him. This made for many awkward family get-togethers.

She was now angry that she had let her father drive a wedge between them, although her feelings needed to be put aside for now. After the conversation she had with her father this morning, April thought he knew more than he was letting on.

He was trying to genuinely help without taking any shots at Mason. She sensed it in his voice and for the first time she could ever recall, he sounded worried. Thinking back to his call, it came in long before any of the news reports had surfaced. He warned her that something big was happening. She still remembered the last thing he said to her.

"Go get Mason and Justin… and the three of you need to leave the city within the hour."

Before she could ask him what he meant, he quickly said he needed to go and hung up.

April wished she would have taken his advice.

13

"What's this?" William asked.

"A pretty effective tool for taking those things down. What did you call them... Feeders?"

"Not my words, internet news started it."

"Here, you get the shiny new one. Try not to bloody it up; I have to train some clients next week."

"Somehow I think you may need to postpone those sessions. I don't think I'll need it though, my house is just up here to the right"

"Keep it... just in case."

As they made their way through the maze of cars that lined the street, Mason noticed people still belted to their seats, unable to escape and who were trapped in their cars when the horde came through. A few cars were still idling and others had their doors half open as it appeared they were trying to flee on foot.

Some of the vehicles were empty, indicating a handful must have escaped. Mason glanced over at

William and motioned for him to stay closer. They were no more than two car lengths apart when Mason felt something pull at his ankle and the next thing he knew he was face down on the pavement staring into the eyes of a Feeder.

This thing was hidden underneath a car and pulled Mason toward itself as he clawed at the asphalt trying to get some traction. Mason felt his fingernails shredding against the street as he kicked his legs, not letting his attacker gain an inch.

He must have let out a gasp as he fell because William was on him instantly, pulling him by his hands as the Feeder continued to pull at Mason's legs. As Mason cleared the underbelly of the car, the Feeder was still holding onto his legs, biting through the fabric of his socks and now almost clear of the car as well. William gave one final pull backward, leapt over Mason grabbing the kettlebell he dropped, and took a long hard swing, pinning the Feeder's head against the rear passenger door.

Mason sat against the car brushing the roadway off his shirt as William came over. "You were right, it DID come in handy."

William extended his hand and pulled Mason to his feet. He shook William's hand a second longer and smiled.

"Let's get home."

The pair made quick work of the remaining maze of cars and were standing in William's driveway with not a soul around, almost as if this street had been untouched by the day's events.

"Mason, it looks like everyone is heading out of the city. What are your plans?"

"I gotta get home to check on my son and my wife, and then I think we are heading out."

"Where?"

"I'm not real sure yet, we're probably gonna head east into the desert where there's plenty of wide open land and try to sit this thing out until the government and military get control of this."

"You want some company... it's just my wife, myself, and my uncle who lives with us."

"Sure, I plan on setting out at dawn. Get your car packed tonight and we'll meet at the corner here... let's say six a.m."

"You want to stay here through the night?"

"I would rather do this when I have some daylight, and the sun is probably going to set in the next forty minutes and I don't want to be stuck in the dark with everyone else."

"Ok, I'm in. Do you think we will be safe in our homes through the night?"

"These things only appear to be alerted by movement and sound. Close all your doors, lock all your windows, and stay inside with the lights off. Be here at six, ready to go."

They shook hands one more time and headed in separate directions. William went up the steps to the front door and turned.

"Mason, how are we going to get around these cars...? We're locked in."

Mason continued to walk and pointed to an empty field just past the cluster of cars. "There's our exit!"

Mason was happy that William had asked to tag along; he felt banding together with another group was good for their survival. It didn't hurt that William wasn't afraid to take action when the time came. Mason also now trusted him.

He's one of the good ones, Mason thought.

As he rounded the corner, he could see the community of his former home just up the road in the distance. He could tell by the destruction around him that this area was also overrun and he prayed as he walked that his family made it back home safely.

As he walked along the sidewalk, there was a crowd of Feeders still roaming the empty school field to his left and they started his way. He began to quicken his pace until he noticed that the chain-link fence separating them proved to be too much. They didn't appear to know how to get over the fence; they just stood at the fence growling and scratching.

As Mason came to the entrance of his development, the line of cars heading out the exit amazed him. He shook his head as he passed car after car filled to the gills with camping gear and family members yelling at one another. They looked as terrified as he'd ever seen.

Approaching the last few cars, he saw his old neighbor John. He waved and John put the window down.

"Hey Mason, I just left April and Justin a minute ago."

"Are they OK?"

"Yeah man, I think April tore up her ankle a bit, but they are fine."

"Thanks John."

"Don't mention it... Just go home and get them out of here, we're heading to Nevada."

"Alright man, take care."

As Mason continued to walk, he noticed garages battered, front doors wide open, and bodies scattered over the first few front lawns. He was confused.

The closer he got to his home, the devastation tapered off to nothing rather quickly. He figured this must be where the neighborhood took a stand or those things only came in as far as they saw something to attack.

Either way, Mason had a feeling of hope. He started to jog up the street and soon he was able to make out his home and what looked like April and Justin sitting in the front yard. He picked up his pace and began to call out their names.

April looked up and motioned to Justin. They saw Mason coming, stood, and started toward him.

14

April appeared to be limping.

As they got to within 50 feet, Justin took April's hand and guided her to Mason and the three of them came together in an embrace. April started to quietly cry as she looked Mason over for signs of trauma. She was pleasantly surprised that he was all in one piece, even though he looked like hell.

Arm in arm they walked back to the house as Mason told them of his escape from the gym and Tom's attack in the parking lot. He left out the atrocious, blow by blow details of his friend's death and how good he felt taking down the Feeders that devoured Tom.

He also described his new friend William and how the two were brought together as William was running from what was once his father-in-law.

They in turn filled Mason in on the events that led to them being chased through the school and seeing the assistant principal being eaten alive. Justin wanted to let his father know how he had helped April across the field and over the six foot barrier that seemed to perplex their attackers and how he was able to handle the two that nearly killed them.

Mason thanked him for protecting his mother and told him that he knew he could do it and was proud of him. Justin also let his dad know he had been trying to text him with no response. Mason reached in his backpack and withdrew the phone, noticing that he had missed five text messages from Justin and apologized for not checking in.

Reaching the house, April swung open the front door and for an instant was caught off guard, but remembered that she had left it unlocked in case Mason arrived first. Mason asked Justin to go around the house and close the shades and turn off all the lights. He carried April into the office since it had no windows to the outside, which he felt would be safer.

As Justin closed the windows in the master bedroom, he paused and looked out over the field he and April had crossed only a short time before. There were hundreds of those things wandering around. The corner of the field closest to the gym was partly lit from the lights serving the parking lot of the elementary school. For a moment, Justin thought he spotted his Spanish teacher among the horde. Whoever or whatever it was turned in another direction and he lost sight of it as it blended in with the others.

Mason checked April's ankle and could tell it was only a slight sprain. Justin hurried downstairs after finishing with the lights and shades. He rested against the wall of the office as his mother and father occupied the small sofa. Mason explained to both of them that it would be completely dark outside shortly and for them to take a quick shower and meet back downstairs. He told April he would wrap her ankle when she was finished.

April stood and looked at him sideways. "Shower... don't you think we need to pack and get on the road right away?"

"Only if you want to sit in line with all the other people waiting for those things to attack. We'll leave first thing in the morning."

"Morning? What if they attack us here?"

"They only seem to come around when the see or hear something. If we keep all the lights off except for here in the office and stay quiet, we'll be fine."

"Dad, I'm getting in now. I'll be out in five minutes. You're on watch," Justin said in his most stern voice.

"Yes, SIR!" Mason replied as Justin trotted off up the stairs.

"Mason, are you sure about this... My dad said we needed to leave hours ago."

"I can't believe I'm saying this, but yes... your father was right. If we would have left hours ago, we would have been fine. We are now stuck waiting for all the millions of people to exit the city... and it's dark, we won't be able to see those things coming."

"I guess you're right, do you think it will be

better in the morning?"

"I sure hope so."

As April slowly made her way up the stairs, Mason sat back in the office chair and flipped on the computer. He searched the internet for any related information that might help them get out of this alive. What little information there was didn't offer any help. There were tons of videos showing everything from crowds of people running from the hordes to the top ten kill shots, all of which involved some form of decapitation.

Frustrated and ready to give up his search, Mason came upon a website that had only become popular within the last few hours. The site administrator claimed to know the cause of the infection. The site was supposedly run by some sort of ex-military Biochemist. He had documents that dated back five years detailing some sort of experiment a privately funded company was conducting on behalf of the military on soldiers in Colorado.

According to this man, the test subjects had their DNA altered through some form of injection that allowed them to stay highly functional for up to five days without the need for sleep and would improve reaction time in combat situations up to fifty percent, among other things.

This Biochemist, Dr. Eugene Lockwood, was sure these experiments were altering the brain functions of the test subjects and he had warned management of impending doom. If he was to be believed, this is why he was removed from the project and was now in hiding.

The comments on his site ranged from people calling him crazy and saying he was some twelve-year-old in a basement somewhere, to a small group of individuals that actually believed every word that was written. They had even begun a campaign to bring this person out of hiding. The last update from the so-called Dr. Lockwood was at 8:30 a.m. this morning. Only two short lines...

It has begun.

Run, Hide, or Fight. NO ONE IS SAFE!

Mason had the feeling that he had heard of this Dr. Lockwood somewhere before and just wasn't sure where. Although he had seen enough tonight, his head was swimming with so many thoughts and he still needed to convince April of the last part of his plan.

As he walked the interior of the house making sure everything was locked down tight, including the garage, Mason gathered a few items and put them in a box. The three of them sat in the office with the lights dimmed as Mason discussed what he had planned for that night.

"There are a few things I need to get from my apartment."

"WHAT...? Mason, you're not serious. We just got you back here. I am not letting you leave."

"We are not taking off until dawn and I'll be damned if I head out into the end of the world in gym shorts and sneakers."

Justin spoke next "Dad that cannot be your only excuse... right?"

"No. There are other things I need. I have a few

guns and they will come in handy."

"A few guns? I didn't know you had any more guns. I thought you only had the one you left here with us?"

"April, you've seen where I live, it's almost a given that everyone in my building has at least one."

"Can't we go by in the morning on the way?"

Frustrated, Mason hung his head for a moment before speaking.

"There are things I have that we need before we leave in the morning. I am not having you wait in the car for me while I am in the building or trying to follow me through there in the dark. I will be able to make it in and out a lot faster if I am alone. I promise to be safe."

April shook her head. "Oh well, if you promise to be safe, I guess that's fine."

"You're no good at sarcasm."

"I wasn't trying to be."

Justin sat in the corner, laughing at his parents' bickering.

April stood up, testing her still painful ankle. "Ok, you BETTER get back here soon or we're coming after you"

"Yes ma'am! I should be back in less than an hour, so I'll shower then."

"OK, what do you need us to do?"

"Get the two emergency kits and the hand-powered flashlights from the garage and put them in the back of the SUV."

"What else?" Justin asked.

"Get all the food that doesn't need to be cooked or kept cold and put it in plastic bags that are easy to carry. Then just a few changes of clothes that fit in a backpack."

Mason continued, "April, get the gun and all the ammo and put it in on the floor in the front passenger seat."

April sat back down on the couch across from Mason so he could wrap her ankle.

"After you both finish packing, stay in the office, dim the lights, and get some sleep. I have a feeling tomorrow is going to be a very long day."

April and Justin looked at Mason and in unison said, "Get some sleep?"

"Well try... for me."

Mason told them to keep everything locked and he would give three short knocks on the door when he got back and for them to check before opening it.

Realizing his father needed to get going, Justin walked over, grabbed his hand, and helped him to his feet. Justin pulled Mason in close and hugged him tight.

"Dad, I love you. Please get back here."

"You don't need to worry about me buddy; I'll be back before you're done packing,"

April took Mason's hand as they walked to the door. She looked up at him and smiled. He smiled back and hugged her. She kissed his cheek and told him to be safe.

He leaned over and whispered into her ear, "If, I'm not back by dawn you need to get to William's house. He'll be waiting at the corner of Morgan and Stone at six a.m."

As he opened the door, April pulled back. "We are not leaving you, no matter what. Do what you have to do, just get back here... fast."

Mason returned her kiss on the cheek, grabbed his backpack and headed out into the darkness.

April closed the door behind him and whispered, "I love you."

15

Not yet twenty four hours into the apocalypse and dark skies blanketed the city. Law enforcement had been completely overrun, power was off in many areas, grocery stores were ransacked and the world was a quiet place. Many hid in their homes or left the city for safer, more remote areas. There were no airplanes in the sky, no vehicles moving about on the streets and the Feeders made their way from one area to the next in a silent death march.

After midnight in this town, there typically wasn't much happening other than the occasional car accident. As Mason made the short trip from the harmless neighborhood he once shared with April and Justin and into the less than desirable downtown area he currently called home, the differences between the two were now less noticeable.

Mason hadn't figured on walking the entire distance between his and April's place, although when he reached his car he remembered exactly where he left the keys and wasn't going back through that mess to retrieve them from the desk in the office. Not only would he be risking his chances of carrying out his plans, he would also have to face April again and he was sure there was no way she would let him leave twice.

He now thought maybe he shouldn't have left them at all...

He was making good time and only had to adjust his route a few times to accommodate going around some of the areas where Feeders were congregating. He noticed that if they heard him, they would start heading his way, although they were easily confused in the darkness by a rock or stick thrown in the opposite direction.

Walking through the park this time of night, he imagined the horde of Feeders at the far end to be an elderly cluster of exercisers out for their early morning jaunt, slowly making their way from one end to the other. He didn't feel threatened by this crowd because they were far enough away and he was able to outrun all the others he had faced that night.

Knowing he needed to stay on schedule, Mason picked up the pace to a slow jog until he came to the end of the park. He had gained the attention of the growing number of Feeders from the park he had just passed through. By his estimation, there were at least twenty of them and they were now headed toward him.

He needed to make a decision. He could go through the alley up ahead that led directly to the rear of his apartment building or go around and use up an extra ten minutes. Mason needed as much time as possible, since he hadn't taken the car and still had to walk back to April and Justin once he got what he needed from his place.

As he got closer to his apartment, the city grew darker. The only light on this side of town was offered by the moon, which much to his appreciation was full tonight. With only one long alleyway to go, Mason started to feel as though his plan may work. He held out hope that what he needed to acquire from the building would still be intact and readily accessible. He prayed it would be.

He decided to head down through the alley and make short work of it. He hadn't noticed any of those things yet and the alley looked clear. Mason couldn't turn back at this point as the group trailing him now filled the area behind him like a cork in a wine bottle.

With only thirty feet to go, four Feeders came from behind the dumpster at the far end of the alley, obviously finished with one meal and looking for their next. Mason stopped in his tracks and turned to see what his options were to the rear just in case they may have started to break into smaller groups.

"Well that's not an option," he said as he pulled the backpack to the side and unzipped it.

Mason decided to move forward and try to maneuver around them with the help of Tom's gun. He slid the revolver out of the bag and started toward them to gauge their speed and to see if they had any injuries that might make this easier. No such luck; although they weren't running toward him, they weren't limping or injured either.

As they approached each other, one of the four noticed something else that caught its eye and branched off to the side. The other three, as determined as ever, stayed the course. Mason wanted to wait to pull the trigger until they were close enough so he wouldn't miss any of them and figured only a head shot would do.

Mason opened the cylinder release to be sure he had enough ammunition, as this particular weapon only housed six rounds. He was happy to see that the single shot he took in the parking lot earlier in the day was the only round spent and he still had five chambered for his use.

With only ten feet between them, Mason raised the pistol, aimed it at the closest of the three and squeezed off a quick shot. The bullet seemed to move in slow motion as Mason watched it enter just to the right of this things nose and exit with a violent burst, blowing off the back of its head. Instantly its body went limp and Feeder number one hit the ground like a huge sack of rice.

The sound of the first shot bounced off the alley walls and appeared to travel to every corner of the city. Mason twisted to the left and fired off round two. This time it sent the Feeder back and up against the wall, a bloody, fleshy mural covered the area behind it.

At the moment Mason squeezed the trigger a third time, the last Feeder still standing stumbled forward over the one lying on the ground. The shot missed and imbedded in the alley wall. The Feeder's momentum caused it to continue to stumble forward and smash into Mason, knocking them both to the ground.

Mason looked around and saw his adversary lying on the ground next to him. When he tried to roll over onto his stomach and stand he felt nauseous. Reaching back he rubbed the sore spot on his head and felt a golf ball sized lump that he must have sustained when he hit the ground. He pulled his hand back and even in the moonlight he could see the blood dripping from his hand.

Mason needed to get to his feet quicker than the Feeder to his right and ahead of the crowd still coming from behind. He couldn't seem to focus and his vision started to go blurry. He knew what was next. He was going to die here in this alley at the hands of the monster slowly moving toward him.

As he started to slide into unconsciousness, he prayed that April and Justin would get out of the city alive.

16

Staring out the bedroom window into the darkness, she could no longer even make out the silhouette of Mason as he made his way through the maze of stalled cars that lined the roads of their neighborhood. April wished she had tried harder to get him to stay, although she didn't want to fight with him. This was the first time in a month they actually talked to each other instead of arguing. It felt good.

Walking back downstairs, Justin startled her as he came out of the kitchen carrying a small box that contained various canned food and light snacks. He was smiling and looked happy. April figured he was glad to have his Dad back, if even for just a few minutes.

"Hey kid, did you remember a can opener?"

Justin made an immediate right turn and headed back into the kitchen. She heard him opening and shutting cabinets and drawers as he searched.

"Top right, next to the sink."

"Thanks mom."

April dug through the closet next to the front door where they kept their winter coats and other items only used a few times a year.

"Justin, where is your old, blue backpack?"

"I left it on your bed. I knew you needed one. You walked right past it."

"Thanks for waiting until I came all the way down here to tell me."

"No problem."

April closed the closet door and turned to walk back to her room. Looking into the office, she noticed a set of keys sitting on the desk in the office.

"Uh OH..."

Justin dropped the box and hurried to see what she was talking about.

"Mom?"

"Your Dad forgot his car keys."

"Uh... So?"

"That means he'll either have to walk back here or make the whole trip on foot, neither are good options."

"You know Dad won't take any chances, I'm sure he will be back here any minute."

April quickly made her way back upstairs to her room and opened the wood blinds as far as they would go so she could pack what she needed and keep an eye on the street below at the same time. She hoped Mason would return and not try to make it both ways without using a car, although she knew better. She knew he wouldn't come all the way back here for the keys, so it would end up taking him even longer. She felt nauseous.

She tried to imagine all the things she would need and wondered how she would fit everything into one small backpack. She thought, "Men could easily do this, although I just need more stuff." She tossed the backpack to the side and grabbed a much bigger duffle bag from under the bed.

"That's better."

Justin continued to make trip after trip to the car in the garage loading everything he figured they would need. He wanted his Dad to be proud of him. Each time he made another trip, he would look out the Plexiglas panes of the garage door, checking for any of those things, and also hoping he would see his father walking back up the street.

He noticed that all the cars were now gone, all the way down to the end of the street. His neighbors must have escaped. He felt a little scared since they seemed to be the only ones left. He had an idea.

Justin ran up the stairs, meeting April in the master bathroom.

"Mom, I'm going to text Dad to see if he's coming back for his keys."

"Good idea. We should have thought of that earlier."

Justin pulled out his phone, hung his head, and tossed it on the sink.

"It's dead!"

"What... no, I charged it last night. Let me see."

April picked up his phone, looked at the screen and immediately set it down. She reached in her back pocket and glanced at hers. She tossed it next to Justin's on the sink.

"It's not dead. The service is down. Let's try the home phone."

Justin picked up the receiver and handed it to April. She listed for a short moment.

"The power is still on, but no dial tone. The phone lines must be down. This is not good; your Dad has no way to get ahold of us."

"Mom, what do we do?"

"Just get the rest of your stuff packed; I'm sure your Dad is fine."

"Ok, I'm done with the food and the stuff from the garage. I'll get my clothes."

"Good. Don't worry, he'll be back soon."

She didn't know if she was trying to convince herself or Justin and who needed it more. April continued to throw together what she thought she would need and tried to come up with a plan for making sure Mason got back here in one piece.

Justin looked back into her room before leaving.

"Mom, all the cars are gone."

"What cars?"

"All the neighbors that were lined up down the street. They are all gone now."

"Good, then we'll get out of here that much faster once your father gets back."

"Mom... Are you scared?"

"Nope."

She wanted to get in the car, go after Mason and

leave the city tonight. She wanted the three of them back together right now. She didn't want to wait anymore. Mason had been gone for over three hours and she needed him. They both needed him.

Justin grabbed an assortment of pants, shorts and shirts. He shoved as many of each as he could into the backpack and zipped it shut. He threw it into the hall and as it hit the floor, the noise made April jump. She quickly rounded the corner and shot Justin a look. It was still rather dark in most areas of the house except for the light coming from the office, although he could tell she wasn't amused.

"What was that?"

"Sorry... just my bag."

"We need to be quiet, remember?"

"Ok, I'm sorry!"

"Justin, what time is it?"

"I don't know, but it looks like the sun will be coming up soon."

She couldn't believe how much time had passed since he left and how long they had been putting their things together. Her nerves were beginning to get the best of her. April was done with this.

She walked over to Justin, wrapped her arms around him and squeezed tight.

"We're going to get your Dad!"

17

The stench of rotting flesh and gun smoke made the air hard to swallow. A candle burned on the empty coffee table in the middle of the room. The faint sound of gunshots grew louder as if it were getting closer.

Mason opened his eyes and tried to focus; his head pounded and he felt like he was going to be sick. He wasn't dead and this certainly wasn't the alley were he blacked out. He had no idea where he was or what was going on. He could tell from the darkness covering the room that sunrise hadn't come just yet.

Squinting through the pain, he saw a figure sitting in a chair only six feet away, head back and eyes closed. As he began to regain his vision, he realized he was lying on the couch in his own apartment. Trying to remember how he ended up here, he looked at the person sitting across the room and through the darkness, recognized the man to be his neighbor.

"Randy, what..."

Randy opened his eyes and lowered his head to meet Mason's gaze.

"Mason! Damn man you had me scared, I thought you were done for."

"How did I get here?"

"I had to drag you here and I mean to tell you it wasn't easy. I couldn't just throw you over my shoulder. You're too tall."

"I don't understand."

"I was up in my apartment and heard a few gunshots right out there in the alley. I looked out of the window and saw that it was you goin' all Rambo on those things."

"Yeah, I guess I lost."

"You never had a chance, there were way too many."

"True, I found out the hard way."

"I rushed down the stairs and barely made it to you right as the big one was climbing on top of you. He went down quick though; I took out the two others that were there by smashing in their heads and then just started dragging you away."

"Thank you, I can't believe...

Obviously excited, Randy interrupted.

"I was only a few steps ahead of them most of the way. They almost caught us a half dozen times."

Mason had only known this man for the last three months and they became friends quickly. He had even gotten Randy a job at the gym, maintaining the equipment. Mason knew he was good with tools and had come to trust him in a way that wasn't easy for others. Randy was only able to hold onto the job for three short weeks before he started showing up late and then not at all. Mason didn't hold it against him and the two continued their friendship without any discussion of the events.

Mason knew his neighbor suffered from paranoia and anxiety due to his stint in the military, stationed in the worst possible places on the planet. He never questioned Randy about the tragedy he must have seen or the horrible things he was made to do for our country.

April only met Randy once and was frightened for Mason, even asking him on many occasions to find somewhere else to live.

Mason wasn't fearful of Randy and in fact felt quite safe living just down the hall from him. He was more afraid of the eighty year old woman living across the hall burning the building down.

Now in his early thirties, Randy began acquiring one weapon after another upon returning from active duty just over eight years ago. He had accumulated a large arsenal that lay just two doors down the hall. The neighbors who knew what he had stockpiled inside his apartment avoided eye contact with him and went out of their way to stay clear, often taking the stairs instead of sharing an elevator ride.

This didn't bother Mason; in fact it was the only reason for him returning tonight.

Mason pulled himself to a sitting position, the nausea and pain starting to subside.

"Randy, you're a big guy, but it must have been crazy getting me all the way up here and into my apartment. I'm impressed... and still alive because of you."

"It really sucked man; took me like almost an hour. I had to keep stopping when those things got close. I would take down a few and then just keep dragging."

"Really?"

"Yep. Once I reached the elevator, it only took a few minutes to get you here."

"You used the elevator?"

"Sure did. Those things get disoriented when it vibrates the building and they actually go in the opposite direction."

Mason owed this man his life for going out into that hell and bringing him back here.

"How did we end up in my apartment?"

"Those things were lined up in front of my door and yours was closer."

"OH..."

Randy hung his head and looked at the floor.

"Mason I had to kick your door in to get us away from those things."

"No worries buddy, I'm grateful."

"I... also... bumped your head again when I threw you on the couch. I needed to get back to the door to close it before they got in."

"Randy, don't think twice about it. You risked your life to get me here and I am as good as new."

"Yeah... well you look like hell!"

"If you hadn't come to pull me out of that alley,

I would literally be IN hell right now."

Mason, at six feet two inches tall and weighing two hundred pounds, had the build of a sprinter. He knew it must have been a nightmare for Randy to haul him around, even with all the training he was given in the military. Mason easily had him by a few inches in height and outweighed him by a good twenty pounds.

"Mason, how's your head?"

"Surprisingly enough it isn't too bad, what is this?"

"I wrapped it and put an ice pack from your freezer on it. The power went out about an hour ago, but it was still pretty cold."

"Randy, I don't know how to thank you."

"No problem man, you'd have done the same for me. You're a good dude Mason!"

"Thanks Randy... for everything."

He needed to get back to April and Justin. Looking out the window he knew there weren't more than a few hours until daybreak and if they were still awake, they'd be worried he wasn't back.

Mason pulled the dressing from his head and winced in pain looking over at Randy.

"Mason, why did you come back? There's nothing here for you."

"Randy, we should get out of here."

"You don't know the half of it. We needed to leave like an hour ago, but why did you come back."

"I'll explain on the way, let's go."

"I haven't even decided where I'm going yet. I

don't really have much family and the ones I do have, I'm trying to avoid."

"Randy, you don't seem to understand. You're coming with us!"

18

The streets had been clear for a few hours. Heat began to rise from the earth, radiating up and creating a thick layer of fog that covered most of the area around their home. April and Justin stared out the bedroom window at the path Mason took on his trip out of the neighborhood.

Justin looked at his mother.

"We're going now? It's still kind of dark outside and the fog is going to make it pretty hard to find him."

"I know, but we have to go."

"Alright, what do you need me to do?"

"Just make sure you have all your stuff and let's get in the car."

"Do you think we will find him? Do you think he is ok?"

"Your Dad is too smart to get caught by those things; he's also too fast for them. You've seen how slow they walk."

"What if he gets surrounded?"

"Sweetie, he's fine, I promise you. He's probably just taking his time. Let's go get him."

She was just as worried as Justin, possibly more. April prayed silently as she gathered the two bags she packed. She hoped Mason was safe and that she would get to him before those things did. Wherever he was, she was determined to find him... no matter what.

As April made her way downstairs, she cursed herself for not being more insistent on him staying here in the first place.

Justin ran downstairs, threw the three remaining bags into the rear of the car and went to the living room window. April came in and stood at his side as he cracked the shades, giving them a view of their front yard and street leading out of the neighborhood.

Groups of Feeders began to form at the far end of the street heading toward their end of the block. April estimated they had less than five minutes to get out of the garage and down the driveway before they had to come face to face with the horde.

Not wanting to see any more or waste any time, April grabbed Justin's hand and guided him towards the garage.

"Let's go."

"Ok mom, where are your bags?"

"Right here, I'll throw them in the back. Grab that flashlight and get in the backseat and lie down."

"Backseat... Why?"

"I want you safe and you don't need to see what I'll have to do if I can't find a way out of here."

"You're gonna run them over?

"Well, I'm not going to let them stop me, that's for sure."

"Go Mom!"

Justin hurried to the passenger side, threw the flashlight in the front seat next to April and jumped into the backseat, knocking over some of the supplies. April moved to the back, opened the rear hatch and tossed her bags next to Justin's. Looking out of the small windows on the garage door, the streetlights lit up the fog and April could see the crowds getting closer. They needed to get moving.

April slid into the driver's seat and sat still for a moment before turning the car over; preparing herself for what she knew was inevitable. She was certain that she would have to run down several of those things on her way out of the area. This was something that wouldn't be easy even if they were attacking her and Justin. These things were human at some point in the last twenty-four hours and some of them she may even have known.

She was going to have to set aside her own humanity, at least until they were out of the city. She may have to do unthinkable things to survive and to keep her family safe. That was her priority for now and nothing else mattered.

"I'm going to open the garage and back down the driveway. Stay down for now... Please."

"I will."

Justin hoped April would be brave enough to do what she needed to do if any of those things got in their way. She was tough in the way that a mother is when you threaten one of their young. He knew she would give her life for his, although he prayed she also valued her own safety as much.

He remembered, on occasion, his mother protecting him from things that would be hard for him to endure both physically and mentally. He wondered if that made him a weaker person because he was sheltered. He needed to be strong for both of them, especially if his Dad didn't return.

As the garage began to open, Justin peeked out the rear window and could see the Feeders getting closer, although they were still far enough away and in small enough groups that he felt they would easily make it out of the area without any real trouble.

As the garage door finished its ascent, April put the vehicle into reverse and slowly began backing out of the garage. She felt as though every muscle in her body was tense and the fear of the unknown began to wash over her again. She checked the mirrors every few seconds as tiny beads of sweat started to form at her hairline.

April didn't want Justin to know she was temporarily falling apart and tried to compose herself long enough the check on him.

"Are you okay back there?"

"Yeah Mom, I'm fine, hurry up!"

Justin turned back toward the garage and looked out the passenger window as they rolled out into the driveway. He spotted something that caught his eye. April hit the garage door remote and continued down the driveway.

"STOP!" yelled Justin.

April slammed on the brakes so hard that even at their slow speed the tires squealed. Her seatbelt tightened, pinning her back against the seat. Frustrated, April tugged at the restraint, trying to free herself as she yelled back at him for startling her.

"Justin, what's the matter with you?"

The words hadn't even escaped her lips as Justin opened the car door and bolted for the garage. He didn't say a word as he ran back toward the house. As he breached the entrance to the garage the sensor detected his movement and the door started back up.

April screamed at him as she put her window down. "Get back here... NOW!"

Justin ran to the cabinets in the garage and grabbed a plastic container from the shelf. He turned back to exit the garage as April continued to yell.

Justin wasn't yet two steps back toward the car when he realized his mistake. Stopping dead in his tracks, he dropped the container at his feet.

Two Feeders had rounded the corner of the opened garage door and were now coming straight at him.

19

The hallways were littered with corpses at various stages of decomposition and Feeders in search of new victims. The majority of the dead stayed down less than an hour post-mortem and as the minutes passed more of them began to rise. The chances of Mason and Randy getting out of the building alive were slipping away quickly.

Mason slowly made his way to his feet, and stood motionless for a few seconds, testing his balance. He asked Randy to give him a second and disappeared into the bedroom, emerging minutes later now in jeans, a tee-shirt and boots. "That feels better."

Randy also stood and walked towards the door.

"Mason, how are we gonna get outta here?"

"I have a plan, but we have to move fast."

"Ok, let's hear it."

"Randy, your place is only two doors down..."

"Yeah, and?"

Mason motioned toward the door.

"From the sound of things, going out into the hall would be a death sentence. I say we bust through these walls instead."

"Won't work."

"Why?"

"Those things may be in the other apartments and even if they aren't it would take hours to get through. These walls are reinforced much more than your average home."

"Really?"

"Yeah, for you know... privacy."

"Makes sense, well what now? We can't go out there."

Randy stared up at the ceiling, thinking of a way out of this place. He walked over to the window and looked back at Mason and smiled.

"Sorry bud, we have to go out there. There is absolutely no other way. We need to get to my place. I have stuff we will need."

"I know... you asked why I came back?"

"I did."

"Randy, I hope you don't take this the wrong way, although I came back to get you. I need you. My family needs you and we need your weapons! When this whole thing went down, you were the first person I thought of."

"Thanks man."

"Don't thank me; I was thinking more about how your special training could keep me and my family safe than I was about your safety."

Randy wasn't offended, hell this was as close to a compliment as anyone had ever given him. No one had ever said they needed him... for anything. Both his parent treated him and his siblings as servants and left them alone every chance they got. His childhood was one bad memory after another. He joined the military the first chance he got and never spoke to his mother or father again.

Leaving the window and walking back over to Mason, the pair shook hands and nodded in a silent bond.

"Mason, you and I are going to leave this building and were going to do it together. Where are April and Justin?"

"At home and probably out of their minds. I told them I would be back in an hour or so."

"That didn't quite happen."

"Tell me about it."

Mason looked around the room and noticed his backpack on the floor next to the couch. Leaning over to grab it, he felt a twinge of pain at the back of his head and winced in pain.

"Still hurt?" Randy asked.

"A little."

Mason dug around in the bag and finally withdrew his cell phone, powered it on and noticed he had no signal. "Damn it."

Throwing his phone back onto the couch, Mason turned and headed to his home phone sitting on the kitchen counter. Randy noticed this and shook his head. "All phones lines have been out for at least two hours, even the landlines."

"How about carrier pigeons, I suppose they all took a leave of absence... right?"

Randy laughed aloud. "Mason, you kill me. How on earth do you manage to still have a sense of humor through all this?"

"It's all we have..." Mason stopped and listened for a moment.

"Randy, have you wondered why there are no sirens? I haven't seen any law enforcement or emergency services since this started."

"Not really, I talked to a cop buddy of mine as this thing was going down earlier and they were getting way too many calls to handle. They called in all the off duty personnel to cover the additional calls and sent the deputies out individually. I'm sure they were just overrun."

Randy walked back to the door and looked out of the hole into the hall. Turning back toward Mason, he still had a smirk on his face.

"How's it look?" Mason inquired.

"The same."

"Then what's with the look?"

"Were going out there, it's the only way. We just have to get to over to my place and stay inside for maybe two minutes, then we are out of here."

"Ok..."

"I'm not smiling; this is the look I get just before I go into battle. It's crazy I know, but that's just the way I am. I hate those things for what they have done and we're going to do some serious damage to them. Aren't you excited?"

"Not really, obviously you are though."

"It's more adrenaline than excitement."

Mason made his way over to the door and stood

next to Randy, putting his ear against the door.

"Yeah, Randy I guess adrenaline might help. How we gonna do this?"

"I have an idea, help me."

Randy moved to the closet door and began to remove the pins that held the hinges in place. He motioned for Mason to hold the door upright as he removed the final pin and set the door against the wall next to the kitchen.

Mason looked confused. "What are we doing, and what's with the door?"

"We're going to use it as a shield. You hold it by the handle and the hinge and push forward."

"Ok?"

"When they get too close and you knock them over or you lose your balance let the door go to the ground and we'll use it as a bridge to go over them."

"Randy, that's brilliant and just might work, what about the ones from behind?"

"Don't worry about it; I'll take care of anything from the rear. They won't even get close. You take care of the ones coming at us from the front. I'll handle the rear."

"Ok, how about the keys to your place?"

"It's unlocked, I made sure when I left. Also, what we need is in three bags in the middle of the living room, so once we get in just grab the big green one and I'll get the other two."

"Then what?"

"Then we're gonna use these."

Randy opened his jacket to reveal two Desert

Eagle 50 Caliber handguns.

"Mason, you know what to do with this?"

"Yeah, but what about the noise?"

"Doesn't matter at this point. We need to get out of here in the next few minutes and without these it won't happen."

"You're right."

Randy looked out, into the hall one last time.

"Once you set the door down and grab the bag, I'll hand you the gun and then we need to head for the elevator... FAST!"

As the magnitude of what they were about to do started to sink in, Mason began to think about the two people he had left behind just hours ago. He thought about never seeing them again and realized they were the only reason he needed to get out of here. He slapped Randy on the shoulder and grabbed the unhinged closet door.

Randy stepped in front of Mason, looked back and smiled one last time.

"Let's go..."

20

The street outside their home still appeared unaffected by the events of the past twenty-four hours, although William knew this wouldn't last. He felt a pressure building inside him that would only be relieved once they were clear of the city and into more open space.

With only a few hours left before he needed to meet with his new friend Mason, William was on edge. His wife Karen had been completely inconsolable since hearing about the loss of her parents. She sat on the edge of the couch in the living room and continued to cry.

William's uncle Joe, at seventy-eight years old, couldn't be of much help. He did what he could and struggled to carry anything heavier than a few pillows and blankets. Joe was at an age where he may end up as more of a liability once they were outside, literally fighting for their survival. The thought of having to care for his uncle and keep Karen safe were more than he wanted to think about right now.

With every trip he made to the truck, William made sure to check the windows for signs that the Feeders were starting to make their way into his neighborhood. This was his only sense of comfort, although he knew it wouldn't last. It was only a matter of time before he and his family came face to face with them, he just prayed it would be later rather than sooner.

On his way back to the garage he stopped for a moment, shook his head and let out a little chuckle.

"Am I really packing for the end of the world? What is my suitcase supposed to look like while I am being chased by deranged, flesh eating half - humans?"

He knew that the only thing he really needed for survival, he and his family didn't possess. For years he had wanted to purchase a handgun that he could keep locked away. With no children in the house, he figured this would be an easy sell to Karen.

He was wrong...

They met in their last year of college and Karen was the most beautiful woman he had ever seen. She was also the smartest. Karen became one of the most sought after negotiators in all of Orange County. In the last year alone she had brokered three of the most lucrative Real Estate deals the State had ever seen. She had a Masters in Psychology and used this to her advantage while in the boardroom. Trying to convince her of keeping a gun in the house was a battle he lost before the thought even entered his mind... and he knew it.

He did still have that kettlebell Mason gave him yesterday as the two parted, although that wasn't going to cut it. William would talk to Mason about stopping on their way out of the city and borrowing a few items from the local sporting goods store. He knew there were only a few that carried guns and was certain that all the gun shops had been picked clean hours ago.

Coming back in from the garage, he noticed Karen was no longer on the couch. William turned into the kitchen where Karen was putting items from the pantry into plastic bags. He stopped just behind her as she turned to greet him.

"Are you..." William didn't even know what to ask her.

"I'm going to be ok."

"I'm glad," he said as he pulled her in tight, the last of her tears running down her face and onto his shirt.

"William, the sun will be up soon. Do you think your new friend is coming back?"

"I know I just met Mason, but I get the sense that he is a good guy, someone I would like to have on our side. I'm sure he'll be back."

"Did you trade numbers with your new best friend?" Karen said with a grin.

This was the first smile he had seen since yesterday morning. William knew it was going to take time for his wife to overcome the loss she suffered less than a day earlier and that she was hiding her emotions for the time being. He knew this was the best she could do for now.

"I think because we were both in a hurry to get home, we just forgot to ask for each other's numbers; although it wouldn't have mattered... the phones are out."

Karen picked up the home phone and listened for a moment before putting it back on the counter.

"If the phones are out, why is the power still on?" she asked.

"I'm not sure. I just hope we make it to sunrise so we aren't running around here in complete darkness."

"William, what did you find online? Were there any answers to what's going on and where we need to go?"

"Not really, most of what's being spread around is just gossip. I don't think anyone knows for sure. The one theory that seems to be running through most of the reports is that this somehow started with the military and that's why we haven't seen or heard any response from the government. It is believed that they were completely overrun in the first few hours and that's why it spread so fast. Big Brother was already knocked down. There is no military or government to help; at least that's what the conspiracy theorists are reporting on the internet."

"Do you think it's true?"

"I'm not sure about anything anymore... well, at least since yesterday morning."

Karen took William's hand and looked into his

eyes. "I know you said earlier that we should head to the coast. Do you still think that's a good idea? I don't want us to get stuck out there on a crowded freeway when those things come back."

"I think it is the best bet we have. If we can get through the mess out there, I believe it will be the safest place to ride this thing out. That way we only have to worry about those things coming at us from one direction."

"Ok, it looks like you put more thought into this plan than I have. I'll help you get the rest of the things into the truck." She paused for a moment.

"William, I cannot lose anyone else... I love you."

"I love you too."

Karen grabbed a few bags and headed out to the garage as William put together the last of the packaged food and looked for more bags.

As she laid the packages into the back of the truck, a transformer at the edge of their community exploded with a shock so powerful that it nearly shattered the windows on the front of their home. The streetlights and the power to every home in the surrounding area were instantly shut down.

"WILLIAM!"

21

It all felt like a bad dream. Everything seemed to move in slow motion and the more she struggled the worse things got.

Tugging at the seatbelt to loosen its grip as she put the car in park, she inadvertently caused the belt to tighten, pinning her back against the driver's seat. With the window already down, April pushed open the driver's door and was immediately met with resistance.

Another group of Feeders had come from the other side of the garage and were now trying to get to her through the window. They began to grab and claw at her as she blindly reached for the button to unlock the seatbelt.

"JUSTIN!" she screamed so loud that the sound echoed through the interior of the car, even with the window down.

The sound of her voice didn't seem to have an effect on those things that continued after her son or the group to her left that she was now trying to escape, even though they were only inches away from her.

Looking out through the windshield, she saw that Justin and his attackers had fallen to the ground. The two fought for position to be the first to reach their newfound prey as Justin scurried backward and got to his feet. The Feeders weren't interested in standing and continued to crawl forward, lunging at Justin's legs.

She had to get out of the car and help her son and the driver's side wasn't going to be an option.

Justin continued to move away until he was stopped with his back against the cabinets. With nowhere to go, he kicked at them as they clawed their way forward, scratching at his shoes. He tried moving to the right and then to the left. He tried climbing onto the cabinets with no luck as they were too high and there wasn't much to get a grip on.

Finally locating the release, April freed herself of the restraint and slid into the passenger seat kicking at the Feeders behind her in the process. She was able to unlock the passenger door and step out into the driveway with nothing between her and Justin but the two Feeders she was now determined to rip apart.

"MOM... HELP!" Justin shouted.

She could hear the terror in his voice that was also evidenced by the look on his face. April's fear for her son had rapidly devolved into anger. She could feel the warm blood start to fill her face as she clinched her hands into tight fists and started for the garage. April had reached her breaking point and she felt a change start to move over her.

She didn't speak another word as she moved quickly to the left side of the garage and grabbed a large metal pipe from the rack next to a bicycle. April looked Justin in the eyes and swung the pipe at the group of Feeders that had followed her from the driver's side of the car and made short work of all three. She was filled with rage and the only sounds she made were the screams and grunts related to the battle she was engaged in.

Justin, now out of time and options, just watched as his mother calmly set the pipe up against the wall and grabbed the first Feeder by the ankles and dragged it to the driveway, pinning it under the car tire.

April quickly returned to the garage and grabbed her weapon. With one hand she pulled the last attacker far enough away from her son that he could get around it and gripped the pipe with the other. She pointed to the car and spoke only once.

"Get back in the car and stay down...NOW!"

Justin hung his head as he walked back toward the car picking up the plastic container he dropped only moments before. He set it behind the passenger seat and jumped in without ever looking back. One Feeder was still pinned under the rear tire. Each time it struggled to get free, it actually locked itself in tighter.

As she raised the pipe above her head, she noticed that this thing on the ground beneath her, desperately struggling to scratch or bite anything it could, was once a very beautiful woman. Thick blond hair covered in blood and debris and deep blue eyes that were barely visible through a milky white haze. April imagined her face was once so beautiful that it could have graced the cover of any magazine. She was now the target of April's indescribable fury.

She wanted to destroy this thing at her feet, she needed to...

A single tear ran down her cheek as she swung the pipe, squarely making contact with the once beautiful woman's skull. It tried in vain one last time to sink its teeth into April's leg as she struck it a second time.

She felt her humanity slowly slipping away with each strike that landed. April felt as though the person she was less than a day ago had slipped down deep somewhere inside her and this new person had taken control of her actions. She was afraid that this new version of her would be void of any feelings or remorse as she acted out her hatred in such a violent manner. Even though this thing wasn't human any longer... it once was.

Landing blow after blow, the monster that lay at her feet had gone limp and was now merely a five foot three inch target for April's rage. She continued to swing harder and harder until her hands cramped and she could no longer grip the piece of metal in her hands. April tossed the pipe to the side, grabbed a hand towel from the work bench and wiped the blood from her arms and face as she walked back to the car.

Justin peered out from the backseat, making eye contact with April. She wasn't sure exactly how much of the last sixty seconds he witnessed, although from the look on his face it was more than she would have liked.

April rounded the front of the car, opened the driver's side and slid in behind the wheel.

As his mother sat motionless in the front seat, Justin watched out the rear window and began to tremble. The number of Feeders heading in their direction continued to grow as each second passed. He knew they needed to move soon or they would have to replay the events of only moments ago, this time with a much different outcome.

"Mom?"

April sat up straight as if being pulled from a trance that held her hostage in some alternate reality. She turned her focus to Justin. Reaching back, April brushed his hair away from his face, pulled him close and kissed his cheek. She finally found the words she needed.

"Never do that again... I mean NEVER!"

22

With the front door not quite open enough, Mason failed in his first attempt to exit the apartment quietly, as the closet door slammed against the door jam. This sent a crashing noise down both sides of the hallway. The route from his apartment to Randy's didn't appear to be too much of a challenge as there were only four Feeders between them. Mason wouldn't look back, as they agreed Randy would bring up the rear and could no doubt handle it himself.

The hall was dark, although there was just enough light filtering through the windows at each end to make the short trip to Randy's apartment doable.

Mason nearly jumped out of his skin as he felt a hand on his shoulder. Stopping dead in his tracks he heard Randy in a hushed tone whisper, "Let's go, I'm right here."

What Mason didn't know was that Randy was about to be put to the test since the majority of the

Feeders were coming at them from behind.

As the pair moved out into the hallway, Randy grabbed the twelve inch hunting knife he had shoved into the drywall outside Mason's apartment. He left it there knowing it would be useful as they exited the building. It proved to be a very effective weapon for eliminating those things quickly and quietly at the same time.

Randy made sure Mason cleared the doorway before he stepped out. He then guided Mason forward continuing to stay close. He knew he had to deal with the growing crowd behind them or they wouldn't have enough time to get into his apartment.

Looking over his shoulder, he could see that there were only a few Feeders that Mason had to get past. Randy decided now was as good a time as any and told Mason to keep pushing forward slowly and he would be right back. Right back? Mason thought. Where was he going?

Taking three quick steps forward Randy shifted his weight to his rear leg and leaped into the air kicking the first in the chest and knocking it to the ground. Two other Feeders tripped over their fallen comrade in the narrow hallway and stumbled to get up. Randy took advantage of their awkward nature and inability to stand quickly. He used an underhand grip, stabbing forward at them multiple times, rendering each one motionless the instant the blade was pushed to the back of their head.

Looking back at his neighbor, Randy saw Mason struggling to maneuver around the small crowd.

The door that they had originally thought would be a good shield simply became more of a hindrance as Mason tried to awkwardly carry it and push their attackers back at the same time.

Randy hurried back to meet Mason as they reached the halfway point between the two apartments and helped him push the barrier as they moved forward.

The Feeders on the other side of the door didn't put up much of a fight as they continued to make progress, even though they were outnumbered two to one. Mason and Randy needed to step up their pace because at the other end of the hall where Randy had laid to rest the four or five lifeless monsters, a new group of those things began to form. They were now climbing over the pile of bodies and the pair didn't have more than ten seconds.

"Drop the door," Randy said.

"Are you crazy?"

"Mason, look back."

Mason turned and saw what he estimated to be eight Feeders. They would be on top of them in just a few moments. He was surprised when he looked back at Randy and saw that same grin he had earlier.

"One last push," Mason said.

The pair dug in and gave one final push knocking down all but one of the Feeders that stood between them and Randy's front door. Mason dropped the door on top of the three that had fallen as Randy slid in front and took out all four attackers, each with a single blow to the head.

"HELP..."

"What's that?" Mason said.

"Sounds like a woman."

"Where's it coming from?"

"Someone HELP me!"

"Mason, it sounds like it's coming from my apartment."

"Let's get in there."

"We have some bigger issues to deal with first... Look"

As the voice continued to shout from the inside of his apartment, the pair turned their attention to the horde now upon them. Mason tried pushing them away as Randy used the knife to try to take them down one at a time.

"This isn't working, we need to put some distance between us and them," Randy shouted.

"OK?"

Randy slashed an arm off one of the Feeders like he was cutting through a watermelon. Freeing himself and dropping the knife to the ground Randy opened his jacket, leaned to the side and withdrew both fifty caliber pistols. He unlatched the safety and handed one of the two weapons to Mason.

"You know what to do..."

"I already said yes."

To Randy's surprise, Mason raised the gun without hesitation and rattled off six quick shots, each one connecting with its intended target. The Feeders went down instantly, one by one, adding to the body count in the hall. The sound reverberated back and forth off the narrow hallway walls and both men shook their heads and rubbed their ears.

Surveying the damage the two had inflicted on their attackers, the place they once called home now looked like a warzone and that is exactly what it had become. Mason figured there must have been twenty-five of those things scattered around the floor on all sides. With the gun still smoking, Mason looked across the hall at Randy and now they both had them same slightly evil and somewhat frightened grin on their faces.

"Randy, I think I get it. I'm not proud of it, but I get it."

"Just don't let all of this change you. Just like you need me for certain things, I also need you. The real you, and so does your family."

"Do you hear that?" Mason said.

"I don't hear anything. This is actually the most quiet it's been all day."

"That's the point. Where's that woman's voice that was coming from your apartment?"

The two navigated through the short maze of downed Feeders and now they stood at the door to Randy's apartment. They both held their weapons tight as Randy pushed open the door, not knowing what to expect.

Sitting in the fetal position, rocking back and forth on Randy's couch was a young woman. She was sobbing quietly and didn't notice that they had entered. She had long red locks and when she finally did look up at both men, the most beautiful green eyes that were now lined with blood-red streaks. Mason instantly lowered his gun as Randy's jaw nearly hit the floor. "Savannah?"

23

The light's flickered for a half second and then the world went dark. While his eyes adjusted to the darkness, William made his way from the pantry to the garage and guided Karen back into the house. Her hands were shaking and damp with sweat. William put his arm around her shoulder and waited as she slid into the seat at the kitchen table.

"Everything is fine; I just need to go check on Joe."

William needed to move quickly and hoped the explosion from the transformer hadn't startled Joe too bad, as a fall at his age could do some serious damage. He didn't want Karen to think he didn't care about her, although if Joe was injured this trip would become a whole lot more complicated.

"William, what just happened?"

"I'm not too sure, but it looks like the lights are off everywhere."

Rounding the corner to Joe's first floor bedroom

William stood in the doorway and couldn't believe what he saw. Joe sat on the bed reading a book with a small flashlight illuminating the pages. His empty bags were still on the floor where William had left them hours before. He was so preoccupied with getting everything prepared that he never checked on Joe to see if he was making any progress.

"Joe, what are you doing?"

"I'm reading. Boy, for a smart guy you ask some pretty obvious questions."

"Why haven't you packed?"

"I don't need to."

"What... why?"

"I'm not going anywhere. You and Karen don't need me and if anything, I'll slow you down and put you in danger. I'm not going to do that."

William knew this was true, although there was no way he was leaving his uncle behind. This man practically raised him and his brother. He wouldn't have become the man he was today without Joe and this was not acceptable. He was coming, even if he had to tie him up and throw him in the truck.

"Joe, you are well aware that there is no way I am leaving you here right?"

"I was afraid you'd be all pig-headed about this and have a deal for you."

"Yeah?"

"I'll go out there with you if you make me a promise."

"Ok."

"If you or Karen get into any kind of trouble, I

want you to take care of each other first. I'm seventy-eight years old and know that I won't be able to keep up in certain situations, so do what you need to do. I know you're a good man and you would do anything for me. Just don't die trying to save me... OK?"

"Joe, we are going to get somewhere safe, somewhere free of all this stuff and you're going to be with us. No exceptions."

"Ok, Ok... I'll get my stuff together and be ready in five minutes."

"Thanks Joe!"

"Don't mention it."

Karen moved away from the table and met William as he exited the hall from Joe's bedroom. They made their way back into the dining room and William explained to Karen that Joe wanted to stay behind and not become a burden to them.

"William, you told him there is no way we're leaving him behind... right?"

"Yes, he agreed to go only if we promise to not put ourselves in danger just to protect him."

"And?"

"And, I told him what he wanted to hear. We really don't have a ton of time to debate what may or may not happen, although that man deserves better than to starve to death in this house or be eaten by those things."

"Your right sweetheart."

"I'm glad you agree."

"What time is your friend supposed to be here, what's his name? Mason?"

"Yes, he should be here within the hour."

"How are we going to time the meeting? I don't think we should just sit outside and wait for him to show up. Do you?"

He prayed Mason would show up and that they could travel as a group out of the city. The thought of doing it on his own made him ill. He had long since lost the opportunity to caravan out of the area with his neighbors and thought Mason's idea of waiting out the initial surge of escapees was a brilliant plan. He couldn't imagine getting stuck in a line of cars a mile long and being overrun by a horde of Feeders. It would be suicide.

"No, I don't think waiting outside is going to be an option. Why don't we finish packing up the truck and you and Joe can get inside and once they get here I'll open the garage by hand and we can drive out together."

"How will we know when they get here?"

"I'll sit in the window of our bedroom and keep an eye out for them rounding the corner to our street and at the same time I can continue to monitor the area for any Feeders that head this way."

"Why do you keep calling them Feeders?"

"It's what the news started calling them yesterday because of the way they attack their victims."

"I know, I just sounds weird."

"It does, but it seems to have stuck. Anyway, let's get Joe and his things into the truck. You can keep him company until we leave and I'll head upstairs."

Karen helped walk Joe through the darkness of his bedroom to the garage and finally into the backseat of the truck. William carried the undersized bags his uncle had packed and secured them along with the remaining items he and Karen put together.

After making sure Joe was comfortable inside, Karen came back around the front of the truck and wrapped her arms around William. She gave him a long kiss and hopped into the passenger side.

"What if Mason doesn't show up by six?"

"He will."

"Humor me."

"If he's not here, we'll go get him."

"You know where he lives?"

"Sort of..."

"Sort of?"

"Karen, don't worry... He'll be here. I know it!"

William pulled the keys from his pocket and handed them to Karen through the open window.

"I'll be right upstairs if you need anything. We'll leave in forty minutes either way."

As he turned to head to the master bedroom, William had a strange feeling that things were going to get much worse before they got any better. He hoped he was ready for what the next few days held.

Entering the master suite, William grabbed a wooden stool from the corner of the room and set it down in front of the bay window. Looking out over the streets leading to his home, things had begun to change rather quickly.

William knew the Feeders would eventually make their way here; he just wished that it would have been a few hours later.

24

The rearview mirror proved to be an unwelcome distraction. The number of Feeders heading toward their house continued to grow at a pace more rapidly than before. April was sure this was due to the events of only minutes ago. She wished that scene hadn't played out the way it did, although they might not be alive if it hadn't.

April looked back at Justin one last time. His eyes were red and tears ran down his face. She didn't know how to feel about what just happened. She wanted to apologize for making him cry; however, he needed to understand that this was not a joke and that they needed to be aware of their own safety at all times. April didn't feel bad. He needed this to sink in and the sooner the better.

As the horde grew closer, April shifted the car into reverse and punched the gas, pushing Justin down to the floor along the backseat. He looked surprised and decided to lay lengthwise and avoid looking out at what his mother had to do.

The rear wheel spun for a second against the lone Feeder April had slid under the tire until it caught traction on the pavement and they continued down the end of the driveway. The car bounced upward when the front tire also made contact with the newly immobile creature. Neither April nor Justin bothered to look back at the house or garage, trying to forget the hell they just encountered there.

A group of four Feeders walked straight into the back of the car as April pulled out into the middle of the street and shifted into drive. They almost looked like bowling pins teetering a few times and then falling to the ground. The car hadn't hit them all that hard; it just looked like their momentum carried them forward even after the car started to move in the opposite direction.

Looking up to the end of their street, April didn't think she would have any trouble navigating around the crowd of Feeders and didn't want to have to run down any of those things as it might slow them down.

As April began to drive forward and mentally plan her path out of the area, the streetlights, blinked and went out one at a time. She could tell that they were only minutes from the sun coming up over the hills and didn't know if the power had gone out in the area or if the streetlights were just powering down due to the coming daybreak.

As they drove down the street weaving in and out of the crowds, Justin noticed that the power was also out in all the homes. Not a single light burned in the entire area and earlier most homes had at least one light on at some point.

"Mom..."

"Yeah?"

"The power just went out."

"I figured."

"What about Dad?"

"The sun will be up in a few minutes and knowing your Dad; he's probably what caused them to go out."

Justin let out a little laugh and kept peeking through each of the windows to see where they were. He was hoping he would see his father walking up the street so the three of them could leave the area together. He wanted his father back, not only because he was worried about him, but also because he didn't like the feeling that he and his mother were alone.

Justin didn't that think he and April could survive another night without Mason. They needed him.

It had become a game of rapid accelerations and halting stops. April had to punch the brakes just as quickly as she started. Weaving in and out proved to be more work than she anticipated. Every few feet there were Feeders bouncing off different parts of the car, a few trying in vain to get a hold of something that they could use to pull themselves onto the car.

"Mom, there are more of them now."

"Yeah, it looks that way."

"Can you go any faster?"

"Justin…"

As April began to pick up speed once again, she slammed on the brakes with both feet coming to a complete stop. She was met by a very familiar face. Tony, her neighbor from only five houses away was standing dead center in front of her car.

Tony had become a great friend. He helped around the house during the few weeks that April and Mason initially split and weren't talking. He was sort of a father figure to her and as he put it, "What else am supposed to do now that I'm retired." He and his wife even brought dinner over during some of April's loneliest moments.

The Tony she once knew was gone now. He had turned. She couldn't imagine the horror he suffered as he left this world to return as one of those things.

Feeders began to surround the car and as each second passed so did their chance of getting out of the neighborhood alive. She knew what she had to do, although the thought of running over this thing that used to be her friend was too much to deal with. The car also couldn't take much more abuse as those things were sure to break a window at any second.

April put the car in reverse and punched the gas pedal. Her old friend climbed onto the hood and started clawing its way toward her. She slammed on the brakes again throwing this thing that was once Tony off the right side of the car. It fumbled around trying to stand as April shifted back into drive and headed down the street.

As she made her way out of the area, April

decided that she wasn't going to stop again until the two of them were a safe distance from those things and this area. She wasn't going to put their lives in jeopardy for anything or anyone. If she had to run down a hundred of those things, she would do it without hesitation.

"Mom?"

"What?"

"Was that Tony?"

"Yes, I didn't realize you saw that. You know, I asked you to stay down back there. I don't want to have to tell you again."

"Ok, I just..."

"Not right now. I have to find that guy's house. The one your Dad met yesterday. What was his name?"

"William."

"Oh yeah."

"Do you remember where your Dad said it was?"

"I think it is just around the corner, on the left."

April turned at the stop sign and pulled the car to a stop fifty feet away from Williams's house. None of the Feeders roaming the area seemed to notice that they were even there.

There was a man sitting in the upstairs window and they figured it must be William.

"Do you think Dad is here?"

"I don't know, but I sure hope so."

"Do you think he sees us?"

Justin hadn't even finished his questions as the man in the window stood and waved. He left the room and disappeared into the house.

"Justin."

"Uh huh..."

"I'm still shaking about what happened back at the house."

"Yeah, I'm sorry. I just..."

April stopped him before he could finish.

"I cannot begin to tell you how careless that was. What on earth was so important that you jumped out of the car and almost got both of us killed?"

Justin reached into the plastic container and tossed a single photo album onto the seat. "This."

25

Standing in the center of the room, both men, now completely exhausted, stared at the beautiful young woman before them. Randy looked over his shoulder at the door and back at the woman. He quickly walked over to the couch, sat down and put his arm around her. He pulled her in close and hugged her tight. She continued to cry and used her shirt to wipe away the tears.

She said, "Randy, they're coming."

"Who's coming?" Mason said.

Randy pulled back and looked Savannah in the eyes. He knew she must have gone through hell to get here and couldn't believe she made it her on her own. She lived over twenty miles away and she hadn't driven a car in years. Her clothes were ripped and stained. Her hands, arms and face were covered in blood and the tears only made things worse.

Had it not been for the events of the last day, Mason imagined that she would have easily passed for a celebrity. He guessed she was in her mid-twenties and from her build, obviously took care of herself. Mason had never seen her here before and wondered who this stranger could be. From the way Randy looked at her; he guessed they were probably in a relationship.

Randy tried to calm Savannah. He brushed the hair away from her face and held her hands in his.

"Savannah, how did you get here? Why did you come?"

"I'm sorry, I should have come sooner. We don't have time. We need to go!"

"Yeah, I know those things seem like they can smell us."

"No, Randy, we need to get out of here right now. Lance and Jason will be here any minute."

"Lance and Jason, why?"

Savannah wiped her face on her sleeve trying to compose herself, then stood and walked to the bags in the middle of the room. She grabbed the smallest of the three and threw it over her shoulder.

"They know about all these guns and other things you have. Don't you remember telling them about it last summer?"

"Yeah, kind of, so what? We haven't talked in months and the last time we did, I almost killed both of them."

"That's the point; they are coming here for this stuff and will do anything to get it... I mean anything"

Mason, now confused just as much as he was

when he entered the apartment grabbed one of the other bags from the floor, and motioned for Randy to help with the remaining one.

"You two can explain who she is and what's going on later. Let's just get the hell out of this building while we still have a chance."

"Mason, I'm sorry. This is my cousin Savannah. Her bothers and I had a really bad falling out a while back and they're coming here to take my stuff. I assume they're armed and won't be willing to negotiate."

"Ok, that's just perfect. We still need to get moving."

"I agree. Savannah, how much time do we have?"

"They brought me with them when they left the house a couple of hours ago. The freeways were a complete nightmare. There are so many dead people that were left in their cars and those things are everywhere."

Randy shook his head. "Where are Lance and Jason?"

"They stopped about a half mile away at that huge store on the corner to get supplies and I told them I would stay in the back of the car on the floor. As soon as they got inside, I popped the hood, pulled all the wires off the distributor cap and ran straight here."

Mason looked surprised. "You made it here without a weapon... all on your own?"

"Getting up to your apartment wasn't all that bad. Those things were too focused on going after you two. I just slid right in during all the commotion."

"Why leave your brothers?" asked Randy.

"They will kill you for what's in these bags and anyone else who stands in their way. I came here to get away from them. I'm afraid of what they have become."

"They wouldn't hurt you. You're their flesh and blood."

"They have already killed a bunch innocent people. They even killed Gene and Joanne earlier today just to get to their stash of guns."

"Are you serious? They're family."

"Yes, something changed in both of them when this all happened. They're like a couple of wild animals. We need to leave... like right now."

Savannah motioned for Randy to stand and turned toward Mason looking him up and down.

"Who might you be?"

"His name is Mason... and he is married!" Randy interrupted.

"I just asked his name. It's not like I want to date him and he's too old for me anyway."

"Thanks," Mason said.

"Knock it off Savannah, it isn't funny. We don't have time for games."

"Alright, alright I'm just trying to lighten things up. I've had a pretty bad day."

"We all have cousin, we all have. Mason, you ready?"

Picking up the gun, Mason dropped the magazine from the gun into his free hand and confirmed he still had enough rounds left to get them safely out of the building and nodded to Randy. Savannah unzipped the bag hanging from her shoulder and rummaged around until she found a gun of her own. She closed the bag, chambered a round and looked up as both men now stared at her.

"Let's go boys. Oh yeah, where are we going?"

Randy, still finishing his preparation, looked around puzzled.

"Yeah Mason, where are we going?"

"My wife and son are waiting for me at home. I told them to leave at sunrise if I didn't return, although I came here on foot."

"My car isn't here either. I had to leave it behind yesterday. How far do we need to go?"

"If we run we can be there in less than twenty minutes."

Savannah looked out the kitchen window and shook her head. "The sun will be up in just a few minutes," she said.

Mason knew his family wouldn't leave him behind, although he was concerned about what they might face if they left the house in search of him.

"Let's go. Once we get to my family, we can all leave the city for a more remote area, maybe the desert and wait this thing out. The more of us that can stay together the better. You know... strength in numbers."

"We're with you Mason," Randy said.

The three walked to the door, bags hanging

from their shoulders. They were ready to once again do battle as Randy took the lead. He pulled a second gun out of his bag and readied both weapons.

"Mason... watch and learn."

26

She knew what it was. She didn't even need to open the cover to know why Justin did what he did. This photo album was a detailed reminder of their life before things went bad. Way before the infection that strangled the life out of their city yesterday. The photos in this album were a connection to her life with Mason from the time they met until their relationship crossed into dark territory.

Every night for a month, April flipped through the pages as she cried herself to sleep. She would tell herself that the next morning would bring a new day and life would get easier without him. It never did. She prayed every night for the two of them to find a way back together, and if that weren't possible, then she just wanted to be able to stop missing him.

April knew this behavior wasn't healthy and finally boxed up the album along with the others in the house and put them in the plastic container her son risked his life to retrieve. He did this for her. He did this for their family. He did this without hesitation. The feeling of disappointment she felt for Justin only minutes ago washed away and all she felt now was guilt.

Tears already running down her cheeks, April unbuckled her seatbelt and silently climbed into the backseat. She kissed Justin on the cheek and explained to him how she regretted losing her temper and not trusting him. She promised never again to take him or the things he did for granted. She finished by telling him she loved him now more than ever.

She grabbed the album from the front seat and set it back in the container amongst the others.

"Thank you."

. . .

William raced down the stairs, through the hall and into the garage, startling both Karen and Uncle Joe. Rounding the front of the truck and opening the driver's door, William stood outside not yet ready to hop in. He somehow needed to get the garage door open and without power, he would have to do it manually.

"They're here!"

"Really?" Karen asked.

"Yes, they are sitting out front."

"You were right. Your buddy showed up."

William took a deep breath, reached up and pulled the garage door's safety release. He ran to the door and quickly pulled up, locking it in the open position. As he moved back to the truck and slid in behind the wheel, Karen handed him the keys. He didn't know what to expect as they exited the safety of their home. He asked his wife and uncle to keep their heads down as they pulled into the street and he would tell them when they were clear.

"What's the plan?" Karen asked.

"I need to talk it over with Mason before we head out. I think I'll drive into that lot across the street. As of a few minutes ago, there weren't Feeders over there. They all seem to have left that area and come in this direction."

"Alright, then what?"

"I'll close the gate behind us. They don't seem to know how to navigate chain link fences."

"You're going to get out?"

"Just for a minute. Once I close that gate behind us, we'll have some time to decide what to do next."

"I sure hope you're right."

"I'm not really sure of anything, although it's our best chance."

William looked into the rearview mirror. "Joe, you ready?"

Joe didn't say a word. He kept his head down, raised his right arm and gave the thumbs up sign. Joe wasn't scared. He was just going through the motions and no longer feared death. He only wanted to help his nephew get to safety any way he could.

. . .

Turning their attention back to the house, April

and Justin watched as the garage door opened and the truck pulled out. April climbed back into the driver's seat and put the car into reverse. With everything that had played out in the last twenty minutes, she had almost forgotten why they left the house in the first place. Her husband was out there somewhere and they needed to find him. She hoped he was just stuck in his apartment, unable to get back to them through the mess that had become these city streets.

As the truck emerged, April was surprised to see a how fast it backed out and down the driveway. William took out four Feeders right away and continued to mow them down as the truck reached the street. They skidded to a stop and quickly started forward in the same manner.

William cleared the majority of the crowd and came to a stop along the driver's side of his friend's car. William motioned for them to follow him and punched the gas once again. Karen lifted her head and looked out the front, afraid of what she might see. To her relief, it was open road down to the lot they were going to meet in.

"Wow," April said as she drove forward behind Williams's truck. "This guy means business."

Checking his driver's side mirror and looking back at what followed, William estimated he would have less than a minute after stopping the truck to jump out and close the gate behind them before the entire horde would converge on the area. He knew it would be close and didn't let off the gas.

April started to worry that she might be following the wrong person. As he accelerated, she thought to herself "What's this guy doing?" She cursed under her breath and pushed harder on the gas pedal to keep up.

As their truck cleared the entrance to the lot, William slammed on the brakes, skidding sideways to a stop and leaving room to his right for his friend to pull in. Handing the keys back to Karen, he jumped out and within seconds was in a full sprint back towards the gate.

As he flew by April, now entering the lot, she was convinced that this man was crazy. He was running back towards those things and nothing he could have forgotten was worth trying to fight them.

Justin had been watching from the backseat and knew what was happening.

He remembered what his mother told him just a short time ago and knew she would be extremely upset, although he could see that William didn't have enough time to do this alone. As he kicked open the door he said, "Mom, I know what I'm doing."

Justin caught up to William at the fence and both pushed the heavy metal gate in unison. William looked over expecting to see Mason and was surprised at how much this boy looked like his father. The two continued to push.

With Feeders only a few feet from them, William managed to lift and then drop the latch closed, locking the gate as Justin let go, narrowly avoiding the grasp of one of those things.

Karen and April had also gotten out and started toward them.

William shook Justin's hand as the two walked back to their vehicles.

"You must be Mason's son, my name is William."

"Yeah, my dad told us about you. Told us about meeting you here."

"Thanks for your help; I wouldn't have gotten the gate closed without you. I figured your dad would have jumped out and helped too. Where is he?"

April approached, her eyes starting to well up as she answered.

"We don't know, he never made it back home."

27

Going back out into this hell that their city had become was no doubt little more than a gamble. The sheer number of Feeders now searching for human flesh appeared to have multiplied tenfold since the nightmare began the day before. Staying in small groups and watching out for one another was the only hope for staying alive, unless you were willing to lock yourself indoors and hope to wait this whole thing out. Mason wasn't willing to do that.

They hadn't really discussed a route back to his home or any sort of a plan for the inevitable conflict they would face if they were to be overrun by a group of Feeders too large for the three of them to handle. Would they split up? Would they run? Where would they meet up afterwards? Thoughts raced through his mind like a freight train on acid as he opened the door, letting Randy and Savannah move into the hallway in front of him.

Their previous battle left a hideous maze of Feeder corpses that proved to be a challenge to navigate. Randy led the way climbing over bodies and pushing aside those he could. The stench that filled the hall was something unimaginable and it took their complete focus not to get sick to their stomachs as they continued toward the east stairwell.

Randy stopped in front of the elevator only halfway down the hall and pushed the call button. As the sound of the bell rang out, Mason looked down the hall and saw two Feeders step out from the last apartment on the right. He looked up at the indicator and could see the elevator ascending, although there were still two floors to go. Estimating that the two monsters heading their way would reach them before the elevator did, Mason stepped forward with Randy to his left and both men raised their weapons and each squeezed off one round.

Randy hit his intended target just above the eyebrow line, knocking Feeder number one off its feet and backwards into the window. Mason's shot obliterated the ear of Feeder number two, although it continued forward not missing a step. This thing was at least six feet five inches tall and had to weigh in excess of three hundred pounds. As its ear was blown into fine red dust, it didn't even flinch. It would be on them in seconds.

As the bell rang indicating the elevator had reached their floor, Randy stepped in front of Mason and fired with both guns at once. The bullet from the gun in his right hand tore through the arm of the Feeder, shattering bone and flesh. It continued forward only another half step as the next round entered through its left eye socket and exited through the rear of its skull with a violent explosion that made the three of them wince in horror.

Savannah checked the elevator and stepped in first, followed by Mason and finally after a few more seconds, Randy.

As the doors closed Mason looked across the spacious elevator and noticed Savannah was shaking and had her head down. Randy asked her to hit the button for ground level and noticed the same thing. Reaching in front of her, he tapped the button with the barrel of his gun and the gears above engaged.

During their decent, Savannah slowly raised her head, blinked a few times and furrowed her brow inquisitively.

"Randy..."

"Yeah?"

"You were in the military for quite a while."

"Ok."

"I read online before my computer died yesterday that this was caused by some kind of weird experiment that the government was doing on soldiers. Do you think that's true?"

"I heard the same thing from one of my old buddies just before my cell lost service last night."

"Well?" Savannah continued.

"Anything is possible. The government has had their hands in things that even scared the hell out of me and I've seen plenty."

Mason's ears still rung as the elevator approached ground level. He checked his weapon one final time as they touched down and glanced over at Randy as he continued.

"We all just better pray this isn't related to Project Lockwood."

"Randy, I'm sorry... did you say Lockwood?" Mason asked.

Before he could answer the doors began to open and they could tell why the upper floors were so quiet. The ground level of the apartment building was crawling with Feeders. There must have been at least fifty filling the lobby like a restaurant giving away free food. They went unnoticed for a few seconds, which gave Savannah time to open her bag and withdraw a gargantuan pistol that looked like it was made to hunt dinosaurs.

Randy turned to her and asked, "You good with that one?"

"Yep."

Savannah checked the magazine in her gun and within seconds the army of three was in position, arms raised and ready to do battle with the horde whose full attention had been turned to them.

Mason took the lead, as Randy brought up the rear. Savannah took out anything that came from either side. "Aim for the head and stay close!" Mason barked over the rapid gunshots.

The trio moved in unison to the exit like a fine-tuned engine laying waste to the numerous Feeders as they approached from all sides. As they cleared the exit, Randy and Mason pushed the heavy concrete bench in front, drastically slowing their attackers. The trio reloaded their weapons and moved away from the building.

They ran into the alley and Mason realized this was where he had almost lost his life only hours earlier. He gave Randy a quick pat on the back, both men knowing the significance.

"Thanks."

"You'd have done the same for me."

With the sun now filtering through the many buildings in the area, Mason checked his watch and realized he should have already been standing in Williams's driveway. He wondered if April and Justin would have left the house and ventured out to rendezvous with his friend or if they were holed up in the house still waiting for him. Either way, he needed to speed things up.

"Hey guys, I think we should head through the park to save some time. I don't think my family will actually leave us behind, I just don't want them out in the open having to wait for us."

As they continued to walk, Randy said, "I agree and we should probably pick up the pace."

Mason and Savannah broke into a light jog with Randy bringing up the rear. They noticed that a couple of large groups of Feeders were headed in their direction as they made their way into the entrance of the park.

"Mason, let's go in over by that wooden platform," Randy said.

"Sounds good!"

They came to a stop just inside one of the entrances that possessed a large wooden gate which was once used as a way to keep vagrants out of the park at night. It was only six feet tall, but most of the homeless never bothered climbing it and moved on to other areas.

Savannah watched for any approaching Feeders while Mason and Randy moved the gate into place. They slid the clasp over the lock just as the horde approached from the other side, narrowly finishing before they were confronted.

"That wasn't too bad. How much farther?"

"Once we get across the park, it's just a few more blocks. Let's go!"

The crack of a gunshot sounded from the far end of the long grass field and they all hit the ground. The top rung of the wooden gate behind them exploded, wood fragments rained down all around them.

Out in the open, they had nowhere to go and nothing to hide behind. Panic began to set in as their attention turned to where the shot originated. Savannah squinted through the daylight now blanketing the area and was the first to recognize their new adversaries.

"They're here, they found us."

"Who found us?" Mason said.

"It's Jason and Lance."

28

Hundreds of ravenous Feeders were only yards away as the group of five gathered in the middle of the empty lot that was the size of four football fields. Only hours before, they were strangers that probably wouldn't have spoken to one another if they passed on the street. Thrown together by fate, they now needed the support of one another to face what came next.

The gate would only hold those things back for so long. These beasts lacked the most basic cognitive skills, including the ability to navigate around anything over five feet tall. Unfortunately they more than made up for it in sheer brutality. They would eventually obliterate anything they came in contact with even at the expense of their own bodies. Nothing seemed to slow the pace at which they pursued human flesh.

William, April and the others made their way through introductions quickly. They discussed what their next steps would be, including where they thought they might find Mason. William explained there was really only one safe way to exit the vacant lot and that was at the far end which led directly into the park. They weren't sure what the open areas inside the park might look like and needed to be sure it didn't lead straight into a large crowd of Feeders.

William asked everyone but April to get back into the vehicles and prepare to leave. He wanted to run down the plan one last time.

"April, you're going to follow me to the top of the hill and once we cross over into the park, we will cut the engines and take a look from up top. We can easily see the entire area from there and plan our route through the main greenbelt."

"Yes, then from there we can cross the field... if it's clear. Mason's building is only a few minutes past the park."

William continued, "That's perfect. We can stop at the other end and reassess before we drive up to his building."

April reached into her bag and handed William the gun Mason left for her. In the past ten minutes, she learned about his past experience as a military medic and figured he would be the best choice to carry it.

"William, you just don't give off that military vibe. I should know, I grew up around it," April said.

"Yeah, it's been quite a while."

The pair made their way back into the vehicles and buckled in for the ride to the top of the hill.

. . .

Randy was the first to stand and locate his weapons. With the bag he was carrying still draped over his shoulder, he moved toward the two handguns he dropped. Bending over to grab them a voice came from the distance.

"Leave it right there Randy! BACK AWAY!"

Randy left the weapons on the ground and took a step back. As they got closer, Randy knew this wasn't going to end well. His two cousins would want everything they were carrying in the bags and they weren't going to leave empty handed, even if it meant killing them.

With only thirty yards left between them, Mason stood and also helped Savannah up. As she got to her feet, Mason slid the pistol he was holding into the back of her waistband and gave a slight nod. She looked back and winked at him.

"You guys ok?" Randy asked. He then leaned in and whispered to Savannah. "I'm going to kill them. I don't know how yet, but they're already dead."

The men, now only ten yards away stopped. The bigger of two, Jason, looked all three up and down, shook his head and smiled.

"Savannah, what did you think would happen by leaving us stranded? You should have put a little more thought into your plan. All you did was piss me off. I'll deal with you in a minute."

Mason interrupted. "Guys, if you're looking for weapons we have plenty for everyone."

Jason turned his focus to Mason. "Exactly who

are you? Never mind, I don't really care. That's mighty nice of you to offer up what doesn't even belong to you. Yeah, we know that beautiful stash belongs to our good old cousin here. We only missed you by a few minutes at the apartment, but here we all are now."

Randy, beginning to seethe, looked over at Mason and shook his head. "Mason, don't give these scumbags the time of day, they're not worth it."

"Scumbags? Really... is that all you got? Even after everything we've been through." Jason raised his gun, pointing it at Mason. "How about I shoot your friend here in the head, will that change your opinion?"

. . .

As they came to a stop next to the camping area that overlooked the park, April and the others exited the cars. The field below was free of Feeders as far as the eye could see. It was as if the events of the past day never happened and they were just a group of friends out for a day of fun.

"Mom, is that Dad?"

"What, where?"

"Look over there, way down at the end with those other people."

April could tell, even from as far away as they were that the groups below were in conflict. "William, I think that might be Mason down there, but... he was alone when he left."

William rushed off to the back of his truck and started digging through boxes, while April continued to keep an eye on the people below.

"Found it," William said.

"What?"

"Binoculars, I knew these would come in handy."

He handed them to April and watched over her shoulder as Justin stood by patiently. She brought the lenses to her eyes and dropped her arms almost as fast as she raised them.

"It's him."

"It's Dad?" Justin said.

She turned to William and handed him the binoculars.

"Look... We have to do something," she said.

William looked and could see right away that it was Mason. He appeared to be arguing with the men directly across from him.

William leaned back against the hood of the car silently thinking of what to do as April continued to watch. She began to tremble as the thought of what she might witness filled her with fear.

"William, one of them just pointed their gun at Mason. I can't hear what they're saying. We need to get down there and help him."

"I don't think all of us charging down there is the best idea; it may spook them into doing something irrational."

William walked back over to the truck and withdrew the handgun April had given him.

"I'm going alone."

"I don't think so," Karen said as she grabbed her husband's face attempting to get him to look her in the eyes.

"Honey, he needs our help and I'll have the element of surprise on my side. Nothing is going to happen anyway, or it already would have. I'm sure it's just a pissing match. Here are the keys, just be ready to drive down when I signal."

Karen hugged William and took the keys. "I'm not going to be able to talk you out of this am I?"

"No, and trust me it will be fine."

29

The grass under their feet was still damp from the morning dew as they now stood face to face with two men, who only hours before had murdered their own family members just for a few guns. Mason couldn't see an easy way out of this, short of giving up everything they were carrying, and even then they may not leave this park alive.

Savannah stepped forward and pulled the gun from her lower back and in one motion pointed it at Jason. She had seen these two monsters cause enough destruction for a lifetime.

Lance now also pulled his gun and pointed it at Mason. "Savannah sweetie, put it down. You're not ready for what comes next. You're soft and I've about reached my limit with you."

"Lance, you weren't that kind of person either, Jason has turned you into something less than human. You two aren't any better than those things behind us!"

"I'll bet I'm a better shot," Jason said. He turned

his head to the side, slid the safety off and fired one round.

The bullet entered Mason's left side just above his pectoral muscle sending him reeling backward and onto the ground. The bag he was shouldering opened and the contents spread across the wet grass. He was surprised it happened so fast and watched as blood began to pour out of the wound.

Jason's stern look turned to a grin. "I was going to try to explain to you how serious I was, but I figured I would just show you instead. Set the other bags on the ground or the next one goes into his temple. NOW!"

Savannah looked back at Randy terrified at what she was about to do.

. . .

"Was that a gunshot?" April cried out. "We need to get down there." She started the car, put it in gear and started down the hill. She could see William now in a full sprint toward the two groups of people less than fifty yards in front of him.

William could see that Mason was down and his assailant was standing directly in front of him. As he continued to run towards them, he raised his weapon and took a wild shot hoping to cause a distraction.

He had no other plan beyond the action he had just taken and hoped Mason wasn't alone in this group.

Grass exploded less than twenty feet away from them. Jason flinched and pointed the gun at Savannah. She instinctively fired on him, making contact in the chest. Jason went down hard, but not before firing back, striking Savannah in the leg and tearing out a good size chunk of her right thigh.

Lance began screaming something unintelligible and started toward Savannah.

Randy slowly picked up the weapon he had dropped earlier and turned it on his cousin now standing over Savannah. She was crying and begging him not to kill her. She said she was sorry and didn't mean to do what she did.

"I'm sorry too," Lance said as he chambered a round.

"Lance, you don't have to do this. She's family," Randy said.

"Not anymore."

Lance quickly turned and fired on Randy, narrowly missing his right ear. Randy didn't even have the time to react before Lance was hit from behind by the second shot fired from William.

Randy quickly made his way over to Savannah and Mason who were both lying on the ground next to one another. As William ran over to them, April and Karen stopped the cars only a few feet away. Mason was the more critical of the two with obvious internal injuries. Savannah's wound was only superficial, although they needed to control the bleeding for both of them as soon as possible.

April jumped out of the car and ran to Mason as fast as she could with Justin right on her heels. She began to cry as she reached him and saw the pool of blood. William had removed his own shirt and placed it over the injury and asked April to keep pressure on it.

"William, is he ok?"

"He's going to be fine, we just need to get them somewhere safe. Mason is very lucky, the bullet went straight through. No fragments."

"Sorry, I was running late. I'm kinda havin' a bad day," Mason said.

"I see that, by the way who are these others?" asked William.

Mason quickly gave them all a rundown of what happened to him after he left the house last night. From being attacked in the alley, their escape from the building and the confrontation with the two men that were now badly wounded and writhing in pain only a few feet from them.

Randy took their guns and added them to what was left on the ground and put the three bags into the back of Williams's truck. He then walked back over to his cousins, leaned over and whispered something only they could hear. Lance spit in Randy's face as he finished.

William left Mason with his family to check on Savannah. He pulled back her jeans to reveal a fairly large chunk of flesh missing. Karen came over and knelt alongside Savannah. She used a towel from the truck as a makeshift bandage.

"You're doing great, what's your name sweetie?"

"Savannah."

"William and I will get you somewhere safe and back on your feet in no time."

Karen had no idea if that were true; she just thought this girl needed to hear those words.

They quickly loaded Mason and Savannah in the car; April drove and Justin jumped in the backseat, taking April's place applying pressure to his Dad's shoulder. William went with them to monitor their injuries and look for somewhere safe to continue to treat them.

William stopped April before she got in the car to leave. "Do you know that huge sporting goods store down by the freeway?

"Yeah, Sportmart... why?" April said.

"Just get there as quickly as possible."

"Are they going to be ok?

"The girl will be fine. She has plenty of time, although Mason has lost quite a bit of blood and I need to get him stabilized and sewn up."

"Alright let's go."

Karen and Joe got in the truck and started the engine. William went over to the driver's window and told Karen about their plan. He told her he loved her, to stay close behind and to flash her headlights if she needed anything.

Randy told Mason to hang on and he would be in the truck with Karen. Mason began to feel lightheaded and as the car started his thoughts ran back to their brief conversation in the elevator.

"Randy..."

"Yeah bud?'

"You mentioned something about Lockwood earlier?" Mason said as his grimaced in pain.

"Sure, Project Lockwood."

"Does that have anything to do with that nutcase Doctor Lockwood?"

"Doctor Lockwood? No Project Lockwood was named after a military base, not a person."

"Oh, Ok there was someone online that said this virus was caused by the military trying to create some type of super-soldier. I figured he was crazy."

"Who?"

"This guy who called himself Doctor Eugene Lockwood. He said he was part of the team that created what eventually became this virus."

Randy couldn't believe what he was hearing. This couldn't be true. How would Mason have so many details about a government-funded initiative that only a handful of high-ranking individuals were aware of. If Project Lockwood was responsible for all of this mayhem Randy prayed the antidote was still out there and being protected. If it was destroyed in all of the chaos of the past day, humanity faced certain extinction.

"Mason, we gotta get going. We're gonna get you somewhere safe and take care of that shoulder."

"Thanks Randy... thanks."

As the enormity of the situation began to sink in, Randy left the group and walked over to his badly injured cousins. He stood over them and fired off two quick rounds, one into the lower leg of each man. Neither of them would be able to walk again anytime soon. They would have to crawl out of this park. That is exactly what Randy had intended.

He leaned in between the two and said, "That's for Savannah... I'll see you both in hell!"

The two brothers wailed in pain as Randy walked back to the truck and withdrew a double barreled sawed-off shotgun from his bag. He fired once at the gate; knocking it off its track and creating a large enough gap that the growing crowd of Feeders started to push through.

Randy placed the gun back in the bag and slid into the passenger seat next to Karen and didn't say a word. He stared out the front window as she shifted the truck into drive and followed April out of the park.

William traded seats with Justin and sat holding the makeshift bandage against his friend's shoulder. He was concerned as Mason's condition rapidly declined and the color began to drain from his face. He knew they didn't have much time and needed to move quickly.

As they turned out of the park and onto the street leading to their destination, William leaned forward and whispered into April's ear. "I need you to get us there in the next few minutes. Mason has lost a lot of blood. It has slowed, but not completely and I need it to. Please don't stop for anything, just drive!"

April didn't say a word; she just pushed the pedal to the floor. She didn't look back. She didn't even check her mirrors, fearing the anxiety would consume her. She just drove, all the while praying for Mason to survive.

William continued to hold Mason's free hand. He gripped it tight, trying to keep him awake. He spoke quietly to him, leaned in and wiped the cold sweat from his forehead. He could feel Mason's pulse had begun to slow and feared their time was running out.

Mason slowly closed his eyes and his grip began to loosen around William's hand...

WHAT'S NEXT?
Book Two – *TURBULENCE*

Turn the page for a look inside the next book in The Dead Years Series.

Also, be among the first to get notified about Jeff Olah's new releases.

Join the mailing list at: JeffOlah.com/Newsletter

1

As they rolled to a stop William looked out over the parking lot from the backseat, shook his head and cursed under his breath. The short distance from their vehicle to the rear entrance of the store would usually be just a short uneventful walk, although the growing horde of Feeders that stood in their way changed all this. With two members of the group having sustained serious injuries only minutes earlier, this was slightly more than they were ready to handle... mentally or physically.

If they even made it to the door, it would take a considerable amount of time to break in. They didn't have the tools necessary to do this and would have to attempt to shoot at the door and hope to blow the lock apart. Making a run at this while trying to fight off the growing horde wasn't going to work. There were too many things that could go wrong and William knew it. He looked down at Mason and cursed again. They needed to get him stabilized and the bleeding stopped within the next few minutes.

As Karen pulled the truck alongside, William looked at Randy sitting in the passenger seat, hoping he may have thought of some way out of this. Randy pounded his fist against the dash and it was obvious from the look on his face that he was just as frustrated. They were both thinking the same thing. There was no way to win this one.

Randy held both hands up looking back at William in a show of confusion. He also mouthed the words "What now." William thought for a short moment and asked April to go around to the front of the building before motioning for Karen to follow.

As they drove forward, the growing crowd of Feeders began to move away from the rear entrance of the building in unison and toward their two vehicles. It looked less like they were hunting and more like they were being hunted. The Feeders appeared to be confused as they moved away from the building and scattered in all different directions.

Looking out toward the horde, Justin couldn't believe what he was seeing.

"WAIT... STOP..."

"What's wrong?" April said.

"Mom, look what that guy is doing."

The rear doors to the sporting goods store were now wide open and there stood a young man holding a fire hose, aiming the high powered nozzle at the confused group of Feeders, motioning April toward him. She smirked at how odd this looked and even though they weren't presently being attacked, she sensed that she needed to quickly head back toward the store.

Karen also turned the truck to the right and headed for the rear entrance following April, now navigating her way through the Feeders.

Heading in the direction of the young man who was still shooting water out into the crowd and over the two vehicles, they pulled as close to the building as possible.

With just enough room to open their doors, Karen and April stopped and looked for their next directive from the young man, who was obviously more focused on what the Feeders were doing than anything else. He looked back and forth out over the crowd, turned the water off and set the hose down. He then ran to the passenger door of the car carrying Mason.

Swinging the car door open, their new friend looked around the car at everyone with his attention coming to rest on Mason. His eyes grew wide and his face instantly began to turn red. He sat in silence for a moment before swallowing hard and remembering the direness of their current situation.

Shaking it off, he looked around the car again and said, "Let's go, grab what you can, they'll be right back on us any minute now."

William opened his door, immediately followed by April, as everyone else jumped out and started to grab what they could. Randy headed to the back of the truck as Karen began stuffing what supplies she could into the bags that had fallen over.

"Hey kid," William shouted.

"Adam... Adam's the name."

"Adam, can you give me a hand over here?"

"Sure thing!"

Adam rounded the rear of the car with Justin only steps behind. Randy and Karen continued to gather supplies from the rear of the truck as April helped Savannah out of the passenger side and into the store.

The Feeders had turned back toward them and were now only moments away as William slowly began to pull Mason's motionless body from the car. The others made it inside with what they could carry as the Feeders reached the truck.

Adam swung in to help carry Mason. He grabbed both pant legs and moved forward as William walked backward, hands firmly locked around Mason's torso. Adam looked as frightened as anyone William had ever seen and he wasn't sure if it was due to the Feeders that were rapidly approaching or the fact that he was staring straight down at Mason.

"Sir, is he dead?"

"No, but we don't have a lot of time," William said.

As they neared the door, William called out. "Randy, did you get the guns, we need some help?"

"Guns... You guys have guns?" Adam asked.

Randy passed the two men carrying Mason as they reached the doorway and said "Way ahead of ya!" He pulled out the shotgun and reloaded it as he moved around Adam and took cover between the two cars.

Feeders were quickly approaching from behind the cars and Randy made short work of them as he fired off two blasts and then reloaded multiple times. Looking back to insure everyone made it inside safely, Randy noticed one of the remaining Feeders had broken off from the pack, making its way around the other side of the car and was nearing the store. He calmly walked over and met it halfway, raised the barrel to the side of its head and squeezed the trigger, spraying flesh and bone fragments against the side of the building.

William guided Adam around the empty racks and boxes that covered the floor until they found a spot to lay Mason on the ground. They found an area of the stockroom where the skylights from the roof were directing their rays right over them. If he was going to get the bleeding stopped, he needed to be able to see what he was doing.

Adam made his way back to the doors and pulled the hose hand over hand until the entire length was back inside. Randy rushed in after him, and closed and secured the doors before the next group of Feeders had a chance to bear down on them.

April was only steps behind, all the while shouting for them to hurry. The tears continued to roll down her face as William began to bark orders.

"April, go with Randy and get as many towels as you can find. Kid... uh, I mean Adam; I need a camping stove and the thinnest hunting knife you can find. Bring it here and fire up the stove."

"Will do!" Adam said.

April and Randy ran off toward the beach

supplies and Adam left for the camping gear. William knew he really didn't need the towels as he was able to find the source of the bleeding and had his thumb pressed into it. He just needed to cauterize the source and sterilize the wound.

Mason's pulse began to strengthen as he blinked his eyes. He screamed out in pain, arching his back as William pushed him back down to the floor. He whispered into his ear. "Stay calm buddy, we'll have you fixed up in no time."

Karen stood behind watching as William looked around in a panic. She said, "I didn't forget," as she handed him the large bag of medical supplies he packed into the truck earlier that morning.

"That's not it," he said. "Where's Joe?"

2

Randy hurried behind April as they began to search row after row for towels. They were in the wrong section and she could see that they needed to get to the other side of the store. Randy had already noticed this and decided to take a shortcut through the racks of clothes that were still upright in the middle of the store. April hurried to catch him.

As they reached the area that used to contain the water sports equipment, it looked like a bomb had gone off in that corner of the store. Beach chairs, water toys and surfboards littered the area. Randy dug through a pile of wetsuits and life jackets with no sign of any towels. April, now down on all fours, sifted through the giant mess of beach and lake gear directly in front of her. Her face began to turn red and her pulse quickened as beads of sweat rolled down her face. Mason needed her and time was slipping away.

"I can't find a damn thing, not one towel. You

having any luck?" April asked.

"Nope, not one towel or blanket or even a tissue."

Panic started to set in as they both got to their feet and looked around the store for another area that may have what they needed.

"Where else can we look?" she asked.

"April, follow me."

Randy took off running and she had a hard time keeping up; luckily it was only a short distance before he slowed again. They almost ran down Adam exiting the camping and hiking area. He grabbed the kid by the arm as he was getting the last of what he needed for William.

"Hey kid."

"Adam!"

"Yeah Adam, where are the blankets?"

"Just behind the backpacks over there," he replied, pointing to the back wall of the store.

"Thanks," Randy said, as he and April moved around the section that housed the kayaks and canoes.

. . .

Pointing in the direction of the exit doors they just came through, Karen assured William that Joe had made it in safely.

"He's over there with Mason's boy helping that young woman who was shot in the leg. Everyone made it inside. I took a head count before we closed the doors."

"Is she bad? I can help, although not until I get Mason taken care of."

"She will be fine. I took a look and the wound is superficial. It looked much worse before we cleaned her up. She just needs it sterilized and wrapped. Joe is taking care of her. You just worry about your buddy here."

As Mason's breathing began to normalize, he opened his eyes and was surprised to see William kneeling over him. He furrowed his brow in confusion and wasn't sure what happened or where he was.

"William... what..."

"Save it. You've been shot. The bullet went straight through and didn't hit anything major. So, we won't need to go digging around for it."

"Ok..." Mason said.

He tried to raise his head enough to look around the room for April and Justin. The pain was just too intense and caused him to lower it back to the floor. William calmly explained that his family had made it there safely as well.

"They're both fine. I need you to do me a favor. What's the pain in your shoulder like right now... on a scale of one to ten?"

"Not too bad, it's kinda numb. Like maybe a five."

"Alright, that's good. You have a pretty high tolerance for pain."

"Why is that good?"

"You'll need it for what comes next."

. . .

April made it to the shelves first and grabbed as many of the fleece blankets as she could carry.

Randy gathered all that remained.

"Let's go," April said.

"Right behind ya..."

As they began to run, April couldn't shake the feeling that she should have insisted that Mason not leave them last night. She ran through the scene in her mind over and over, each time cursing herself for not being more firm. She told herself that if she got him back, she wouldn't let him leave her ever again.

She stopped running, turned and stared directly into Randy's eyes. There were no words that could match what she was feeling at the moment. She wanted to speak but couldn't.

"April... I'm sorry for what happened to Mason. I know that you have never liked me and I don't blame you. Mason is here because of me and I will do anything I can to make this right."

"Make it RIGHT? You wanna make this right. Go fix him... Go fix him right now. I want my husband back. I don't care about anything else. Just FIX him!"

Randy didn't speak again. He put his head down and started toward the stockroom again where William was tending to Mason.

Coming through the door first, Randy laid the blankets next to William. April followed and moved to the other side of Mason. She knelt down and whispered into his ear. She squeezed his hand and told him that she loved him. She said she was sorry for everything that happened in the past and would never again let anything tear them apart.

William desperately needed to get started. "Randy, please take everyone out into the store and look for supplies we can use out on the road. Karen is going to help me stop Mason's bleeding and I don't want anyone here to distract us."

"Sounds good... Let's go," Randy said.

Justin stopped long enough to give his father a kiss on the head, grabbed his mother's hand as she stood and walked out of the stockroom.

Joe took Savannah's hand and the pair followed the group, limping out into the store. Savannah wasn't sure if she was the one being helped or if she was the helper as Joe seemed to struggle to even keep up the slow pace at which they moved.

William looked over at Adam as he held the blade of the ten-inch hunting knife over the open flame of the camping stove.

"Did you remember to wipe it down with the rubbing alcohol first?"

"Yes sir."

"Good, is it ready?"

Adam held up the knife, pointing out the tip. "I think so?"

"Great... I'll take it from here. You can head out there with the others."

"Ok."

Adam handed the knife to William and made his way to the doors.

"Adam."

"Yes?"

"You did great kid," William said.

"Thanks."

Karen took the spot earlier occupied by April and sat on the ground. She took Mason's hand, looking into his eyes. "Sweetie... my name is Karen and I'm going to help William fix you up. You're in good hands."

Mason tried to focus on what she was saying as the pain came rushing back. "Thank you."

William held the knife over the flame a few seconds longer as he looked back at the wound for his target. Once he found it, he moved his left hand away replacing it with the red-hot tip of the blade. Mason screamed out in pain and closed his eyes once again.

Karen looked up and shook her head. "He passed out."

"Yeah, I know. That's good."

"Why is that good?"

"Because I lied to him. There is still a fragment of the bullet in him that I need to dig out."

3

The doors swung open as Mason's scream bounced off the interior walls of the store, causing everyone to turn. Their attention now on the stockroom, the group watched as Adam came through the opening alone. April was afraid to ask what was happening since she wasn't sure she really wanted to know the answer. She had only left his side moments ago and was trying to ease Justin's worries about his father, even though his concerns echoed her own.

Randy sat on the floor, checking on Savannah as he talked with Joe, making introductions and small talk. He asked about William and Karen and the initial hours of the outbreak. He loved the way Joe told the stories and felt an instant bond with him. Randy never seemed to care very much for the older men in his life, starting with his own father all the way up to his superiors in the military. He hated being talked down to, but Joe appeared genuinely interested in what he had to say.

"Randy, those were your cousins that caused all that mess back at the park?"

"Yeah and her brothers," Randy said, motioning toward Savannah.

"Stepbrothers... and they were terrible human beings before all this madness. What happened yesterday just turned them into monsters, they had no remorse." Savannah said.

"So, you two are actually blood related?"

Savannah smiled. "Yes, and if it weren't for him I'd probably be dead right now."

Randy raised an eyebrow and also smiled. "I'm glad you're ok, but I know you can take care of yourself when you need to."

. . .

April met Adam as he moved out into the open area behind the aisle of running shoes with Justin right behind her. She knew he wouldn't have much information about Mason; it was too soon for that, although he may be able to fill them in on what was going on inside the stockroom. She hated having her husband's life in the hands of two people she'd known less than a day, even though they were his best chance.

"Adam... that is your name, right?"

"Yes, and you guys are April and Justin?"

"Yeah, my husband is the one they are working on in there. You wouldn't happen to know how he's doing... would you?"

"Your husband seems incredibly strong. I think all they're doing is making sure the bleeding is stopped. He's going to be fine."

Adam had no idea if this were true, although he knew they needed to get the bleeding stopped and this woman looked like she needed some good news.

"Adam, thank you for everything. If it weren't for you we'd still be out there looking for somewhere to hide from this mess."

"No worries, I needed you all too. I was beginning to think no one would come by and I'd be stuck here."

"Well, you're kind of stuck with us now."

"That's good because the last of my co-workers took off earlier today and never came back."

. . .

William shifted to the side, letting the slightest sliver of light shine into the wound as he lowered his head next to the Mason's shoulder and searched for the small piece of brass still remaining. Karen continued to hold Mason's right hand as she dabbed her husband's forehead every few minutes, keeping his sweat from dripping into his eyes.

"Karen, how's he doing?"

"His pulse is getting stronger, although he passed out again. Is that because of the pain?"

"Yes, I think so, although his pain tolerance is unbelievable."

"Did you get the bleeding to stop?" Karen asked.

"Yes. It had almost stopped on its own already. I cauterized it just to make sure. I just need to get this last piece out and sew him up before he wakes up again. Did you thread the needle?"

"It's just to your left... in the pan."

"Thanks..."

William took a deep breath and steadied his hand as he slid the blade of the knife gently under the fragment and withdrew it without touching any part of Mason's exposed flesh on the way out. Setting the blade to his right, he reached over turning off the still burning stove and let out a sigh of relief.

Karen smiled and wiped his brow once again. "You did great seeing as how you haven't been around any of this in years."

William let out a little chuckle. "Yeah, it's been quite a while. Just like riding a bike though. Now let's sew him up. You ready?"

"Sure. He's still out. Is the wound still clean?" Karen asked.

"Yes, I made sure to sterilize it twice."

William took the stainless steel pan containing the two needles that Karen threaded and set it on the ground to his right and just above his injured friend's shoulder. He asked Karen to let go of Mason's hand and to be ready in case he woke up.

They rolled Mason onto his side and made short work of the exit wound, stitching up the entire length in just a few minutes. Surprisingly Mason remained motionless, as William thought he certainly would have already come to. They covered their work with the makeshift bandage William fashioned from medical tape and gauze and then slowly rolled him onto his back again.

William pulled back what remained of Mason's

shirt, nodded at Karen and began to thread the needle back and forth through the skin on the entry wound, carefully pulling each strand tight. With only two passes of the needle left, Mason began to twitch and moan. Karen moved in over on top and gently held his shoulders down. Mason began to kick his legs and scream out in agony.

"Hold him steady," William said as he slid the needle through the skin and pulled tight once again.

She was fighting a losing battle from her current position, so Karen slid up onto Mason's stomach and pushed his shoulders back to the ground, just as her husband pulled the thread tight, trying to finish the job. Mason lurched forward, breaking the thread and sending the needle rocketing toward a pile of boxes in the corner of the stockroom.

"William, tie it up. I can't hold him down any longer."

ABOUT THE AUTHOR

Jeff Olah is the author and creator of the best-selling series The Dead Years and The Last Outbreak. He writes for all those readers who love good post-apocalyptic, supernatural horror, and dystopian/science fiction.

His thirst for detailed story lines and shocking plot twists has been fueled over the years by stories from Cormac McCarthy, Ray Bradbury, and Stephen King. He also has a difficult time tearing himself away from character driven dramas like The Walking Dead and LOST.

He lives in Southern California with his wife, daughter, and five-year-old Chihuahua.

Connect with Jeff:
JeffOlah.com
Facebook.com/JeffOlah
JeffOlah.com/Newsletter

Also by Jeff Olah

THE LAST OUTBREAK

A companion series build in the same world as the Best-Selling Post-Apocalyptic saga *The Dead Years*.

No one knew how or where the end of the world started.

Ethan Runner was hungover, pissed off and once again late for work. He didn't care about anything or anyone, but that was about to change; it had to.

Six days ago there were reports of a mysterious illness. People were actually attacking and devouring one another. The world was told not to worry, that there wasn't a reason to panic, that these were isolated events.

This morning the human race found out that this was a lie.

The infection took hold quickly and destroyed everything in its path. Millions perished every hour. Was this nature's way of thinning the herd, or was this something much more disturbing?

The Last Outbreak follows Ethan Runner, a clinically depressed armored truck driver, as he and a small group of strangers fight through impossible situations to free themselves and one another from this hell.

AWAKENING is the story of their survival.

Hold on... this is only the beginning.

Made in the USA
Lexington, KY
26 December 2016